BY THE RIVER

Buckham is a pretty little village on the banks of the Thames, where Joanna has lived all her life. Her father, Jock, has a successful luxury car dealership, and the family home is McAllister Lodge, built by Jock as a monument to his status. When her father dies, Joanna's world is turned upside down. First her best friend, Laura marries the man that Joanna has always loved. Then her father's business goes bust and Joanna's comfortable existence comes to an end. She knows she must learn to stand on her own two feet, but what does the future hold?

BY THE RIVER

BY THE RIVER

by

Rose Boucheron

Magna Large Print Books
Long Preston, North Yorkshire,
BD23 4ND, England.

British Library Cataloguing in Publication Data.

Boucheron, Rose
   By the river.

   A catalogue record of this book is
   available from the British Library

   ISBN 0-7505-2140-6

First published in Great Britain in 2002
by Judy Piatkus (Publishers) Ltd.

Published in Large Print 2004 by arrangement with
Piatkus Books Ltd.

Magna Large Print is an imprint of Library Magna Books Ltd.

Printed and bound in Great Britain by
T.J. (International) Ltd., Cornwall, PL28 8RW

Chapter One

Joanna McAllister made her way along Buckham High Street recognising many people she knew and acknowledging them, for everyone knew the McAllisters. She was very pretty, with her dark, shiny hair and vivid green eyes – everyone liked Joanna; she was friendly and always ready to stop and talk.

Not today, though; there were more pressing things on her mind as she made her way to see her friend from schooldays, Laura Troubridge that was; since her marriage, Laura Woodward.

It was a fine spring day; everyone seemed to be in a good mood after the rain which had steadily poured down for days had at last stopped. The streets were fresh, the florist's shop was alive with spring colour, there were even a few tourists around early this morning as she approached the heavy glass door of the gallery.

Buckham was a small, pretty town on the River Thames, where it lay within commuting distance of London, thus making it a popular choice for celebrities and the rich who desired a house in a beautiful setting not too far from town. The High Street straggled from the main road through the town until it reached the river, upon whose banks sat an exclusive hotel and a rather nice church of some earlier date.

The High Street had plenty of shops which catered for the local clientele, who knew what they wanted and whose needs were great: expensive boutiques, shoe shops, picture galleries, a fresh fish shop – unusual these days – plenty of pubs, three antique shops, and latterly a supermarket, which the residents had strongly objected to, but were now only too pleased to accept.

The best antiques shop in the town was owned by Giles Troubridge who had inherited it from his father, James. Not many browsers entered; they patronised the two cheaper shops, but his showroom was always a joy to behold. Full of the finest furniture, porcelain and ornaments, it held pride of place in the town with its Georgian façade. Most of Giles' business was done by people requesting a particular article, or by being told that he had something in the window that would interest them. For Buckham was encircled by some of the finest houses in the district. They rose up into the Chilterns, and were mostly owned by famous television personalities and the extremely wealthy who could afford the luxury of these properties, sometimes mansions, with surrounding land which afforded them privacy.

Giles Troubridge, now in his late seventies, lay ill at his home, Heronsgate, not too far out of the town, where it sat in two acres of landscaped gardens. The shop itself was managed by an assistant, Martin, a sixty-year-old ex-employee of the fine arts house where Giles had trained, and at odd times by Giles' daughter, Laura, a young married woman, who had done her training in the same house.

When Laura had married, Giles had moved out of Heronsgate into the large and spacious flat over the shop, while Laura and her husband Simon took over Heronsgate.

As a girl, Laura had been one of the lucky ones. Never having had to work, she tried modelling, and achieved a minor success, but she hated the world she found herself in; and then she tried acting, at which she was no good; then a course at both Sotheby's and Christie's, followed at her father's request, which did nothing to inspire her to take over the business.

Now, three years on, her father was seriously ill. He had moved back to Heronsgate, where latterly he was attended by a nurse, and Laura had had to accept that his illness was terminal. He lay now in his bedroom, which faced the river, a tall gaunt man, ravaged by the illness which was slowly killing him, his eyesight fading, but still able to see the view faintly. If he put his glasses on he could see the river way below him where on a sunny day it sparkled like a string of diamonds. It was his favourite view – he had been born here. On fine days in the summer, trippers and tourists took river trips, sailing past the splendid homes where boats sat tied to the jetties which led to manicured lawns and picturesque houses. England at its best, they told themselves, and nothing pleased them more than to hear the skipper announce as they passed the name of the people who lived there. Ooohs and ahhs, and open mouths – such peace and beauty, such magnificence – such money.

He fretted and worried about his only daughter. What would she do when he had gone? What would happen to the business? For it was fairly obvious that she had no real interest in it and only worked in the gallery to please him.

It was Martin's day off, and Laura sat in the shop, bored as she usually was. Not much business was done by the odd browser, although one woman did buy a Georgian footbath – for flowers, she said. She looked like a typical television personality, Laura guessed: tight leather trousers, white polo neck sweater, little boots with heels that looked a foot high – at least to Laura – and the ubiquitous long, blonde, stringy hair falling over her face, which bore not a scrap of make-up. Laura dealt with the credit card, and assured her that the footbath would be delivered the next day. Thank God for Martin, she thought.

Back at Heronsgate, things were looked after by Mrs Lawrence, the housekeeper, who had been with the family for some years, with help from a local woman, Nell Dorgan, who also helped to clean the brass and silver in the shop, but had warned Laura that she wouldn't be able to carry on much longer, as it was all getting too much for her.

'I'll keep on at your Dad's as long as I can – but I'll have to give the shop up, I'm thinking. I'm sixty-seven next birthday–'

'You're not!' Laura exclaimed. 'You don't look it, Nell.'

'Well, I feel it sometimes – the old aches and pains–'

'What about your daughter – Mandy – doesn't she work for the Davenports?'

'Er – yes, well, I don't know, I'd have to ask her – anyway, not to worry – I'll keep going for a bit. I'm not going to conk out just yet.'

Laura wished she was at home. It was so boring working in the shop. She could have brought a book with her, but somehow she couldn't concentrate on reading. She browsed through some fine art journals. Perhaps her friend Joanna would call in – she did sometimes on a Thursday.

She and Joanna had been at boarding school together, as luck would have it both coming from Buckham. They had been good for each other although they were so different.

Sometimes she didn't know what she would do without Joanna. She had been such a friend to her all along, especially when she had battled with her father about what she wanted to do – and again when she had wanted to marry Simon. What a battle that had been. Her father had hoped she would marry someone in the antiques world, but it was not to be. He never seemed to get it into his head that she had not the slightest interest in the fine arts. What would she do when her father died, as he would soon, without a doubt? She had never really been good at anything – impatiently, she got up and went over to the window, and saw Joanna coming towards her with her swinging walk, her head held high.

Laura smiled, a big grin, and opened the door. 'Oh, Jo, I'm so glad you've come–'

The girls hugged each other and Joanna dropped into the nearest chair. 'I've only popped in for a minute, I've just been shopping,' she said.

'Where's your car?'

'In the car park... How is your father?'

'No change – still the same.'

'Poor old man,' Joanna said. She was genuinely fond of Giles Troubridge.

They were very different to look at. Laura was tall and fair, like her father, willowy, almost, while Joanna was shorter, dark-haired with green eyes – and when she remembered these days, a lovely smile. Laura thought Joanna looked tired: there were circles under her eyes as if she hadn't slept. She wondered if everything was well with the family business; she had heard rumours – but she wasn't going to mention it if Joanna didn't.

'Is everything all right?'

'Yes – why?' Joanna asked swiftly.

'Nothing – just that you look tired.'

'I feel fine,' Joanna said.

'Is your mother well?'

'Seems to be. I haven't seen much of her lately – I was on my way there when I thought I'd pop in to see you. How's Simon?'

'Well, in the States to promote his new book – back tomorrow.'

Joanna hoped she didn't look as awful as she felt – but she certainly didn't intend to bother Laura with her troubles – she had enough of her own to deal with.

Laura nudged Joanna. 'Jo! Look–'

Joanna stared out of the window and saw passing by on the other side Lady Davenport and her two daughters.

'Look at her,' Laura said. 'Dressed to kill. There's no holding her since Sir got his title.'

Joanna laughed out loud. 'And those two awful daughters – they don't get any better, do they? Do you remember them at prep school?'

'Do I?' Laura said grimly. 'And they're just the same – stuck-up bitches.'

By now Lady Davenport had passed.

'Well, how about coming for a meal?'

'Darling, – I can't.' Laura got the impression that Jo was hedging.

'I know, I mean, it's not much fun at home with Dad so ill, but you could pop up and see him – he'd like that – and you know what a fab cook Mrs Lawrence is–'

'Well, I'll see what I can do. Actually, I must go and see Mum – it's ages since I've been. I really only called in for a moment to see how you are.'

'You know I'm always glad to see you,' Laura said getting up.

Joanna picked up her handbag and made for the door. 'I'll ring you,' she said. 'Regards to your father.'

'Bye, Jo.' Laura said as the door closed behind her.

Joanna walked back to the car park. She was glad Simon hadn't been there. She still found it difficult, after all this time.

Her mind harked back to when they had first met. Laura had been in the south of France at the Troubridge holiday home near Nice. She had been there often enough herself. But that year, she had gone with her

17

parents down to Cornwall, where her father kept a boat – both he and her mother were mad on sailing. Joanna was not so keen, much to their disappointment, and had come back early. She had had a week to herself, playing tennis, swimming, and had enjoyed it enormously – and then she had met Simon – Simon Woodward.

She couldn't have said what it was about him that made her heart beat faster each time she saw him. He was an author – a novelist – with one bestseller to his name, and he said it was the devil's own job to repeat the success he had had. He was taking a few days' break before getting back to it.

Joanna and Laura had their own little crowd; they both had swimming pools, tennis courts – life was very good for them, and there were always hangers-on. But this man, Simon, was different. He had the same kind of background, and came from Henley, where he lived with his father, a surgeon.

That week Joanna thought was the best of her life. She was almost twenty, and had never met anyone before to disturb her heart until Simon came along. Whether he felt the same about her, she had no way of knowing, for they were always in a clique and couples were always pairing off. She only knew that she was so excited when Laura was expected home – couldn't wait to tell her of the new addition to their little circle.

There were about six of them in the garden, on a hot sultry August evening, when Laura came home. She looked lovely, her fair hair swept back, her blue eyes sparkling – she was in white, all in white, and she was staring at Simon. Joanna looked at her, startled, then at Simon; he too, seemed mesmerised. She told herself Laura often had that effect on men, but it was not often that Laura herself was affected.

Feeling a strange emptiness in the pit of her stomach, she took Simon's hand and led him over to meet Laura. 'Laura – meet Simon – Simon Woodward,' she said, and she saw Simon take Laura's outstretched hand. Then both pairs of eyes looked away – or seemed to be dragged away from each other – and Laura leaned forward and kissed her.

'Darling – Joanna–' she said. 'I've missed you.'

'Welcome home,' Joanna said – and knew then that she had lost him.

So much water under the bridge, she told

herself now, getting into her car and driving herself towards McAllister Lodge.

A week later, old Giles Troubridge was dead.

It was a shock, although they had been expecting it. He had died in the small hours, the nurse said; she hadn't heard a sound. He had just slipped away. God was merciful, she said. Now, she made him presentable for his daughter to see, the doctor had been called, the certificate presented. It was time to talk of a funeral.

Laura shut herself up in her father's little study and wept, great racking sobs, until she dried her eyes and felt completely wrung out. On the desk was a photograph of her mother, who had died when Laura was fourteen, a beautiful woman, and pictures of Laura herself with her father, horseriding, by the river, in the garden, and Laura and Simon on their wedding day, and everywhere around the room, the watercolours that her father was so fond of.

It was up to her to decide about the funeral, she knew, and Simon would leave it to her. There was no one else. Her father had heaps of friends, business and otherwise, and she knew if they all attended the funeral what an enormous affair it could be. She felt unable to cope with it. A quiet funeral, with just family and later a memorial service – later when she felt she could deal with it.

Her father had had two sisters, both with families, and there were some distant relatives in Canada and France and the United States. She would get in touch with them – but it was unlikely that any of them would make the long journey.

Martin was a tower of strength. He helped with the funeral arrangements and with the notice for *The Times*.

The funeral was a small, sad affair, followed by a light luncheon back at Heronsgate which Mrs Lawrence and Nell Dorgan had prepared. Afterwards, when the guests had gone, Simon took his wife in his arms. She had never felt so utterly alone.

'Darling – you must be brave,' he said softly.

She broke away. 'Oh, what do you know?' she cried.

The Davenports passed the cortège on their way home. Lady Davenport sat beside her daughter in the Mercedes. Louise was at the wheel while Helen sat at the back. They were both very pretty girls, but not as beautiful as their mother, whose good looks were spoiled by a permanent frown and a pained expression. Now she leaned back, her eyes closed.

Louise glanced at her. 'All right, Mummy?'

'Yes, dear,' came a small voice. 'I'm all right – just tired.'

'Get you home for a nice cup of tea.'

Julia Davenport made no reply. A deep crease between her fine dark eyebrows betrayed the fact that she was worrying about something, but then that was not unusual. She owed her beauty to her colouring. Her hair, which had been jet black, had turned white when she was very young and now it was a soft silver. Her mouth was well formed, the lips full and luscious, but fretful, pouty, the corners turning down. Her nose was fine and straight; her eyes were remarkable: round eyes of a deep violet, they were fringed by long lashes. Her skin was smooth and firm and slightly olive-tinged. She was a hypochondriac of the first order – had been all her life.

When Louise operated the electric gates, the car swung up the drive to the big house, which sat overlooking the river. The garden was massed with flowers – Julia Davenport was a flower-arranger of no mean order, and the grounds were immaculate.

They let themselves in and dumped their parcels in the splendid kitchen.

'Ah, you're still here, Mandy. I thought you were going at two-thirty?' Louise asked.

'Yes, I was, but Sir Dennis telephoned to say that he will be coming in early and is off to Paris immediately – and I wondered if you wanted me to do any packing, M'Lady.'

'Oh, how kind – yes please,' Julia said, frowning and dropping into a chair. 'Oh, what a nuisance, just when I am not feeling so good–'

Three pairs of eyes looked at her, as she closed her own. 'My back is killing me – and I have such an awful pain – here–' A delicate hand with long, dark, painted nails lay over her heart.

'Oh, dear,' Helen said at length, just as the sound of her father's key turned in the lock.

Sir Dennis came in, a big handsome man, well over six foot tall. 'Hallo, girls – darling–' He went over and kissed his wife, but she didn't open her eyes. She looked so pained.

'What is it, darling?' he asked her.

'Oh, don't worry about me,' she said

23

faintly, and opened wide brave eyes to his. 'I'll be all right.'

'Did Mandy give you the message? I have to be in Paris this evening.'

She gave a little moan, and the two girls watched.

'Darling, perhaps I had better not go? Have you phoned the doctor?'

'Oh, he won't know what to do – he's such a fool,' she said.

'Where is the pain, darling?'

'Here,' and she took his hand and pressed it just below her breast.

'Look – Louise – get hold of Stamford – tell him to come round at once.' He looked down at Julia, whose eyes were still closed.

'I won't go–' he said. 'I can't leave you like this–'

'But darling–' Her voice was faint.

He held up a hand. 'No, it can wait – now tell me–'

Louise went out to telephone, raising her brows at Helen as she did so, but Helen refused to meet her eyes.

Finishing her telephone call, she met Mandy in the hall.

'Oh Mandy, you can go,' she said. 'My father isn't going to Paris – Mummy is not well.'

'Oh, very well. I'll be off then,' Mandy said and went to get her coat from the kitchen.

As Mandy walked down the drive she thought, there's one born every minute.

Chapter Two

Three weeks after Giles Troubridge died, Joanna ran all the way from the narrow terraced house to where she had parked the car along the road in a lay-by, breathless and stumbling until she reached the door of the car, her fingers trembling so violently that she could not turn the key. Then she was inside, collapsing into the driver's seat, her heart thumping wildly, fighting for breath, waiting for the shaking to stop and her heart to slow down. She seemed to sit there for hours when a tap on the window startled her, and a woman's face was pressed against the glass, mouthing 'Are you all right?'

She nodded stupidly, like an automaton, calmer now, and her arms folded round the leather-covered steering wheel. She was not surprised to find her face wet with tears.

After a while, her heartbeats grew steadier,

and she relaxed against the soft leather. Where had she gone wrong?

Reliving her life up to now, soul-searching, no easy answers came. But she felt steadier, calmer, and knew she must go home. But where was home? Saltlake Cottage where she and Adam lived? Or half a mile away, where her mother lived at McAllister Lodge – except that she would not be there now; she would be at the office, which was just as well – she didn't need pity or want consolation. Least of all– 'I warned you...'

She took a deep breath. If only her father were alive – but then perhaps none of this would have happened. Her thoughts were still in the past.

McAllister Lodge was set high above the river in Buckham, and named by her father when he and her mother, as new parents, first built it. Jock McAllister was a man larger than life, a household name in the world of automobiles. Big, handsome, charming – he had it all. Her mother told her that when he was a lad he was the finest mechanic in the Midlands, but it was the prestigious cars he liked, the smooth perfection of them, their performance. It was not long before he opened a garage, then another, and knew after a time that he must come south to London.

When he opened his first car showrooms in Park Lane, he was deemed to have arrived, and no one knowing him earlier would have been surprised. Her mother had worked for him as his secretary, then when she became pregnant, they married and built the house in the Chiltern Hills with a fine view of the river. Like everything else he did, it was perfection. A pool, landscaped gardens and a four-car garage, a Mercedes, a Bentley, an Aston Martin and a scarlet Porsche which he gave to his daughter on her twenty-first birthday.

'I hope you realise how lucky you are,' her godmother said. 'You were born with a silver spoon in your mouth, that's for sure.'

For of course, she was. There was nothing she wanted that she couldn't have. Her father adored her; he had always wanted a daughter, her mother said.

So she grew up with everything she desired: a prestigious boarding school, a finishing school; there was a tennis court, a swimming pool, heaps of friends, and she was attractive, she knew. She had all the clothes she wanted, and every girl knows how that helps. She even had a special friend of her own, Laura Troubridge...

And then she met Simon Woodward...

She could bear to think of it now, but it had taken a long time. It seemed ridiculous; she had only known him a week, yet it was long enough to believe that he was the only man for her; she had fallen hopelessly in love with him. With Laura's return from France had come the rude awakening. For he and Laura had been drawn to each other like magnets from the moment they met, and yet she would have said Simon was not Laura's type.

But she had been wrong; for six long months she had had to sit back and watch the affair progress as it did relentlessly until they were married. A wonderful wedding, as she stood by and watched – thank God she had not been asked to be a bridesmaid...

They settled down at Heronsgate, Simon to get on with his book and Laura to help her father out in the business.

A year after they were married, Joanna met Tony.

Tony Hargreaves. What could she say about him? How could she sum him up? He was her male equivalent, she supposed, the son of wealthy stockbrokers, and he really was handsome. Tall, well built, with dark eyes which could set a girl's heart on fire, thick black curls no amount of cutting could curb; he was athletic, swam, played tennis – and rugby. He lived for rugby, it was his passion, so he had not much time for girls, but what he had he spent with her.

Her father was delighted.

'Joanna,' he said, 'nothing would please me more–'

'I know, Daddy,' she said, 'I know.' She had no doubt that they would marry – hadn't she always got what she wanted?

It was after the tennis-club dance that Tony proposed, looking down into her deep green eyes, his strong, tanned arms about her – he made her feel so fragile. 'Let's get married,' he said. 'What are we waiting for?' and he bent and kissed her.

Her heart fluttering like a bird, she couldn't remember what she said; she only remembered that he took her to the best jeweller in town and bought her a magnificent solitaire diamond.

The first person she told was her friend Laura Woodward. 'Oh, that's wonderful!' Laura cried.

After that, the McAllisters and the Hargreaves got together and planned the wedding. Joanna was happy enough to go along with it, she had what she wanted, the second prize, and it was quite a wedding. There were hundreds of guests, her gown (French couture), the pearl headdress, the string of pearls (Daddy's wedding gift), the matching earrings (from Tony), a honeymoon in the West Indies, and back home to Saltlake Cottage, a house owned by Tony's father, which he gave to them as a wedding present.

She liked being Tony's wife, and the little cottage was sweet. It had all mod cons, of course, their parents had seen to that between them, and her father insisted that Molly, their maid of all work, should give a couple of hours a week to Joanna, so there really wasn't much to do. Joanna played golf a little and saw a lot of Laura and her other girl friends, who were all envious, mainly because she had managed to marry Tony, the ultimate prize.

She was disappointed after two years that she hadn't started a baby; still, as her mother said, there was plenty of time, they were young yet.

Tony worked in the City and the hours were long – he started early in the mornings, so for Joanna it was a long day.

It was on their second anniversary that Tony had first came home really drunk. In fact his friends had carried him home from the rugby club. 'Sorry, Joanna,' they had said. 'We thought we'd better get him home safely–'

Before that he had often come home the worse for drink but not as bad as that.

Joanna – they – coped with it, not wanting anyone in the families to know.

She used to think: if only I had a baby – something to take her mind off their problem, but she said nothing, not even to Laura, about Tony's drinking. She soon began to realise that he was an alcoholic, and he needed help. But he pushed any mention of that aside – and they grew more and more estranged. Joanna, because she felt sickened with what had become of their pretence of a marriage, and Tony, because deep down he was ashamed.

Feeling guilty because she knew Tony had been second best, and wondering if he had realised it and that been the cause of his drinking, at the end of another miserable year she had been to specialists to ask about her non-fertility. She had always had irregular periods, and now they told her there was little likelihood of her conceiving without an operation, but there was no guarantee even then. She felt at this point in time she wanted to take no chances.

Her parents found out first about Tony's drinking problem, and urged her to leave him, but she was loath to do so, hoping he would give in and go for treatment. However, he was too proud.

The night came one November when he was arrested for being drunk and disorderly and then three nights after that, while she was helping him to bed, he lashed out and hit her.

She went home to her parents – it was the worst night of her life.

There followed a divorce, and soon after that, her father died suddenly from a massive heart attack, leaving her mother quite bereft, but Linda McAllister picked up the pieces and went back to her old job as secretary to McAllister's.

As Joanna came to terms with her life, she realised that she had lost all interest in men. Her mother often despaired, telling her one broken marriage wasn't the end of the world, but it seemed so to Joanna. Laura was a great help during this time, but life wasn't too easy for her. Simon spent a lot of time in town and she had the business to run and an ailing father.

Eighteen months after her divorce, Joanna

met Adam – tall, rangy Adam, a mechanic in the workshop – and eight years her junior. He was repairing her Porsche, and the first thing she noticed about him was that he didn't seem to resent it being hers. A lot of young men felt it was wasted on a woman.

It started from there.

One evening after work she asked him if he would like to go for a drive. He seemed doubtful, but she persisted. 'Why not?'

'Well–' He was young and a little shy.

'Oh, come on,' Joanna said. She was used to getting her own way.

So he came and they went for a drive. The second and third time they even stopped at a country pub for drinks.

When Joanna came in from the pub, she found her mother standing by the kitchen sink with her arms folded. 'Joanna – what on earth do you think you are playing at?' she asked.

'What do you mean?'

'You know very well what I mean,' she said. 'That young boy–'

'Adam?' Joanna asked.

'Yes, Adam – from the workshop,' her mother stressed.

Joanna took a deep breath. 'I like him,' she said. 'What's the harm? He enjoys a ride in the Porsche – he's nice–'

'I expect you mean well,' Linda McAllister said, shaking her head.

'What?'

'Well – it's just not suitable – I mean, he's an employee – a mechanic–'

'So was father,' Joanna said.

Snobbery was not one of her mother's vices, but Joanna knew what she meant; she also knew that she did not intend to give up seeing Adam. He was quite the nicest man she had ever met. Kind, considerate, gentle, all the things, in fact, that Tony had never been, and she enjoyed being with him. The age gap didn't seem to matter, at least not to her.

His family lived in Mitcham and on one of their evening jaunts they called in. His mother was welcoming, an Irishwoman from Co. Kildare, warm-hearted and kind, with three younger children, and the house was small and cosy – in truth, Joanna suspected the kind of house her father had come from. They invited her to stay for supper – she thought it was great.

They became closer, obviously, even though Adam demurred sometimes. 'You should be finding yourself another nice husband,' he said on one occasion, with the faint trace of Irish accent that he still had.

'Does it worry you that I'm that much older?' she asked him.

'No – more that you are the boss's daughter–'

She knew after some months that she was not going to give him up. She knew that she was truly in love. Every moment she was with him was a joy.

They moved into Saltwater Cottage, Joanna's now since the divorce settlement, and Linda McAllister, facing the inevitable, gave him promotion to the showroom where, perhaps not surprisingly, he did very well. He was tall, young, good-looking, and he knew cars inside out and backwards. He was also honest, a rare attribute in a salesman.

Even her mother conceded that he was quite an asset to the firm, but she still couldn't get used to the idea that Joanna hadn't made the perfect marriage to such an eligible catch as Tony.

The main reason they didn't marry was Linda McAllister. Joanna knew it would break her heart. She so wanted her to be her father's daughter, successful, happily married to the right man. Joanna thought they were on the right road, she was blissfully happy,

Adam was doing well at McAllisters...

A year after they had been together, Adam mentioned a baby. Joanna was thirty-two by now and Adam twenty-four. Her heart sank. She wanted nothing to come between them. They were so happy, he was wonderful about the house and garden. She thought they were both as happy as Larry.

'Oh, darling,' she said, fearful at the thought of what she might have to have done.

'I was hoping by now you might be pregnant. Do you think we might have a problem? Perhaps it's me,' Adam said ruefully, looking at her with his kind grey eyes.

'You're really keen,' she said.

He looked surprised. 'Yes – aren't you?'

'I'm happy as I am, but if you want children–'

'I suppose coming from a big family–' he said. 'Poor little you – no brothers or sisters–' and he gave her a bear-hug.

She played safe, and said no more. Waited until he mentioned it again.

What happened during the next few weeks was that he became quieter and didn't laugh as much. He would become irritable, which was so unlike him. Perhaps, Joanna thought, it is this baby thing. Perhaps I should tell him that I have to have – but she put it off, yet again.

One afternoon she called in at McAllister's to see her mother, and found her in the showroom with a client. She waited until they had finished, then her mother went to the cash desk, where a little red-haired girl sat at her counter behind the safety grill. She gave Joanna such a malevolent look it took her by surprise. Some of the staff were envious, she supposed, of her position; not unnaturally, saw her as the boss's daughter. Then Adam walked in, and seeing her there looking at Alise (that was the name pinned on the girl's jacket) he blushed a fiery red and the girl and he exchanged a look which Joanna thought she would remember to her dying day.

She found herself hurrying out of the accounts department and almost running upstairs to her mother's office, where she flopped into a chair, feeling quite sick. It couldn't be! Adam wouldn't do that to her – that girl – what was she – nineteen or so – oh, and her cheeks burned. How would she face him this evening? But she was trembling all the same. She excused herself and went home after lunch.

That evening when Adam came home she knew by his face that there was something wrong. He was pale, and there was a nerve twitching in his cheek. He went upstairs to change, and when he came down he poured their usual glass of wine.

'Joanna,' he said. 'I have something to tell you. I don't want to hurt you – but–'

'That girl,' she said and the words sounded harsh and grating.

He reddened. 'Don't blame her,' he said. 'It was my fault. I'm sorry – but I think it is time that we–'

'Split?' she said. 'Is that the word?' Then she broke down and wept, and threw herself at him. 'Oh, don't leave me, please, Adam, please don't go – I couldn't bear it.' And being Adam, he hugged her tight and comforted her and later they went up to bed and made love, and they said nothing more to each other, but he looked so troubled, she almost wanted to comfort him. 'I really didn't want to hurt you–' he said, and when she woke in the morning he had already left for the office.

She went later to McAllister's, into her mother's office. One look at Joanna and Linda took off her glasses and said, 'What's wrong?'

'It's Adam,' Joanna said. She hadn't intended to say anything, but somehow it came out.

Her mother didn't seem in the least surprised. 'He's got someone else,' she said.

'You knew?' Joanna stared at her, horrified.

'It was inevitable.'

'Why? Why?' Joanna asked her. 'We were as happy as sandboys.'

'So you thought, Joanna poppet.' She came over and put her arm round her daughter. 'Let him go, darling. He's young, he deserves a young wife and family – he's a nice boy–'

'Never!' Joanna said. 'He needs me – I know he does. He needs me!'

Linda put on her glasses again and went downstairs to the showroom. 'You're being very selfish,' she said, as she left.

Selfish! Joanna couldn't believe what her mother had said. She sat there, doing nothing, going over and over the events of the last twenty-four hours. She knew Adam was taking a special delivery down to Wiltshire, an Aston Martin to an Arab tycoon, and wouldn't be in until late.

She went up to the second floor to the personnel department and looked up the record of this Alise Willoughby – yes, she was twenty, joined the firm six months ago – lived in Willesden. Well, she would see about that. She would talk to her, explain – take her darling Adam away from her? Never!

That evening, it took her ages to find Alise's house, all round the back streets, but she did eventually. She parked the car in a lay-by and walked back to number forty-seven – a neat little Edwardian villa, with railings in front and a cat lying by the gate. She knocked at the door, her heart hammering loudly. She didn't know what she expected to achieve, but she would talk to this girl, make her understand.

When the door opened, the wind was taken out of her sails. She was totally speechless. The girl was the prettiest little thing, very young, and away from her counter not very tall – but hugely pregnant...

Joanna ran – stumbling all the way back to the car.

Born with a silver spoon? Silver-plated, more like.

Chapter Three

Joanna had passed Saltwater Cottage and was now on her way to MacAllister Lodge, up the winding lane where the autumn leaves were changing colour and blackberries filled the hedgerows. But she saw none of this, and as she approached the gravel drive, saw that the doors to the garage holding the Aston Martin were open and the car was missing.

She frowned, and glanced at her reflection in the car mirror. God, she looked awful: her eyes were red-rimmed, she looked years older. Her face was drained, and she hurriedly put on some lipstick. She had no wish to shock her mother.

She sat back for a few moments in the car to gather some strength. What kind of reception would she get from her mother? She knew she would get no sympathy. And at the end of the day – what? It was over, finished. No amount of loving on her side would alter the facts. That little girl was pregnant and with Adam's baby. There could be no doubt about it. Perhaps if she – but no, face it, if she had not been prepared to go to any lengths to give him what he wanted... She felt like crying again – couldn't bear to think it was really over. After last night – she wasn't really a cruel person; a spoiled one, perhaps, but she really wouldn't wish any harm to that girl – or even the pair of them. No use crying over spilt milk, her mother would have said. Spilt milk – she took a deep breath and, getting out of the car, locked it.

She inserted the door key in the lock and heard, before she got to the kitchen, the muffled sound of sobbing. Hurriedly, she pushed open the door and saw her mother sitting at the table, her hands to her face, hiding her eyes, while opposite sat Ted Lavers, the company manager. He had one of her mother's hands in his and was comforting her. They both started as Joanna walked in, more shocked than she liked to show.

'What is it? Mummy? What's wrong?' So seldom did she see her mother upset. She was strong – always had been. She hurried over to her and Ted quickly took his hand away from hers. 'Your mother's upset,' he said tersely. He had not much time for

Joanna, thinking her spoiled and lacking consideration for her mother.

Joanna sat down beside her and took her hand. 'What's wrong? Tell me.'

When her mother shook her head, Joanna looked at Ted. 'Where's the Aston Martin?' she said, looking from one to the other.

Her mother looked up. 'It's gone – sold,' she said simply.

'Daddy's Aston? What do you mean – who to?'

Ted took her mother's hand again. 'Linda – tell her. She's got to know sooner or later. Why are you protecting her?'

Linda dried her eyes, and blew her nose, then looked straight at Joanna. 'We – McAllister's – is bankrupt. We're finished. The Aston has been sold – to the Arab client – Adam has driven it down to Wiltshire.'

'Don't you ever read the papers? Have you not noticed what a bad state the economy is in?' Ted's voice held a sneer.

'Of course I did – but–'

'You thought it didn't affect us? McAllisters? We're the first kind of firm to be affected – luxury cars.'

'But I thought–'

'Your mother keeps everything from you, protects you like she always has done – well, it's about time you learned the facts of life.' He got up and went over to stand by the window.

'Don't go on at her, Ted, she's got troubles enough of her own.' Tears sprang to Linda's eyes.

Joanna sat, feeling ice-cold, trying to absorb what Ted's words meant. McAllisters finished? But–

Linda got up and went over to put the kettle on. 'I'll make us a cup of tea – we can do with it.'

'I'll go now,' Ted said. 'But I'll be back later–' he turned to Joanna '–And you look after your mother; she's going to need all the help she can get. See you later, Lin.'

The door closed behind him. Joanna stood, dazed for a moment – one shock after another – then quickly crossed to her mother, putting her arms round her.

'Mummy, I had no idea–'

Linda looked sad, then furious at the same time. 'This is what comes of spoiling you – everything you've ever wanted, no thought for anyone else – you're living in cloud-cuckooland with that boy–'

'It's finished,' Joanna said, now feeling empty, drained. 'Over. That'll please you,' she said bitterly.

Linda put her arms round her. 'Oh, darling, I'm not sorry. He wasn't for you. But now you are going to have to be brave – we're in a mess.'

'What does it all mean?' Joanna asked, eyes wide.

'We're broke. The receivers will have to be called in – McAllisters will be no more – I can't bear it, for your father's sake.'

Joanna felt the tears well up again. 'Did Adam know?'

Linda shook her head. 'He might have had some idea – but, no, he wouldn't realise the extent of it.'

'Poor Daddy. Perhaps it's a good thing he is not here to see it.'

'Perhaps,' her mother said, her lips set in a straight line. 'All these years, wasted, gone. All for nothing.'

'No, not for nothing,' Joanna said quickly. 'It's all been worthwhile – all of it. This lovely house, the cars – we lived the life of Riley, I suppose and now we have to pay for it.' She tried to grin.

'You have no idea what you are talking about,' Linda said severely. 'There will be no house, no showrooms – no cars, no money, nothing.'

'But they can't take everything, can they?'

Joanna said, horrified.

'I'm afraid so. And you've been so protected all your life. You didn't even have the benefit of your dad's and my upbringing. That would have shown you a thing or two, I can tell you. Now it's gone, all of it.'

She gave a weak smile.

'You'll be all right, you'll have the little cottage; it was bought and given to you by Tony's father and then of course you got it in the settlement. But you won't have much more than that. Just your own possessions, and any money you might have.'

'But Mummy – what will you do?'

'Well – Ted has been a brick; I don't know what I'd have done without him. The thing is – I'll tell you now, we've been seeing each other for the last few months.'

'Ted!' Joanna was shocked.

'Yes, he's a nice man. I think, if he is still willing, we have a future together. I shall have nothing, but he had already asked me to marry him.'

'I had no idea,' Joanna said slowly.

'Well, darling, you have been wrapped up in your own affairs.'

'Life with Tony wasn't all that wonderful.' Joanna's eyes clouded over.

'No, darling, I'm sorry, it hasn't been easy,

and now, you say Adam has gone–'

'I went to her house,' Joanna said shortly.

Linda put her hand to her mouth. 'You didn't! Oh, Joanna.'

'Well, I don't know what I thought that could do. She's pregnant, very much so.'

'I know,' Linda said.

'And you never said.'

'I see her every day, and I knew what was going on. And he did tell you he wanted to leave. I knew how upset you would be. And I also knew that it would right itself eventually. Things do, you know.'

'Perhaps you are right. He wasn't for me, that's obvious.'

'You're young. You must look to the future. You'll find someone else.'

'Never.' Joanna sounded adamant.

Linda gave a wan smile. 'You will.' She went over and made the tea. 'Well, we have a lot to do, and I am glad in a way you are free to give all this terrible business your attention. After all, you're very much involved. All the business side, Ted and I will see to – there's a lot to be done. I must put the house on the market, but I thought after the house is sold, perhaps I could come and stay with you for a bit, before–'

'Before–'

'Before Ted and I get married – then I'll move in with him. When it's sorted.'

Joanna took her mother's hand. 'I wish I were half the woman you are,' she said.

'We spoiled you,' Linda said. 'Gave you too much, too soon. But you've not been all that lucky, and my God, in this world you do need a bit of luck. Money isn't everything.'

'I'll stay here tonight,' Joanna said. 'All right?'

Linda smiled. It would be like old times.

The first person Joanna called round to see was Laura. She had seen little of her since her father's death, knowing how busy she would be, immersed in business affairs.

Wednesday was early-closing day although many shops stayed open these days, but Laura took advantage of a free afternoon to close shop and see Joanna. They had so much to talk over.

She threw her arms around Joanna. 'Oh, I am so pleased to see you. It's been awful – still is–' and she held Joanna away from her. 'You look pretty grim too. What's up?'

'You may well ask,' Joanna said. 'Anyway, your news first. How's it going?'

'Well, not too bad, really. Martin's been a brick all through. Nurse has gone, of course, and Mrs Lawrence feeds us well–'

'What are you going to do? About the business, I mean?'

'It's early days yet, and we'll carry on for a bit while we sort things out. But I'm getting rid of it, Jo. I don't want this millstone hanging round my neck – it's too much of a worry, and my heart isn't in it. It's a pity for Daddy, but he knew how I felt about it. Martin can't afford to buy it, he says the business is too big; and the idea is that the stock will be purchased by my two relatives who have shops and we'll put the shop itself on the market. Sad, but there it is.'

'Well, it is a shame when you think how long established it is, and the goodwill and everything.'

'But it means I would have to be in charge – there's no one else – and I simply don't want it, Jo.'

'Yes, I can see your point.'

'Daddy knew this, which is why he was so upset – sending me on fine art courses, and all that. My heart just wasn't in it.'

She glanced up at the clock. 'It's a bit early for wine – how about some tea? There's a good cake here Mrs Lawrence made. Now Father has gone, she misses him. He loved home-made cakes,' and she bit her lip. 'Nell

– Nell Dorgan will be leaving anyway – says she's had enough cleaning silver to last her a lifetime. I don't blame her. She's getting on a bit.'

She looked hard at Joanna, who certainly wasn't her usual self. 'Anyway, what of you? May I say you don't look one hundred per cent – and I mean that kindly.'

'It's a long story,' Joanna said. 'I think I need that tea – here, let me pour.'

Laura cut the cake. 'Well?'

'I don't know quite where to begin. With the important stuff I guess. McAllister's has gone bust.'

'What?' So the rumours had been true. Oh, poor Joanna – and Mrs McAllister. 'Is that definite?'

'Positively and irrevocably,' Joanna said.

'How terrible. Your poor mother. How is she?'

'Coping. You know what she is. She has explained to me what will happen. Everything must go. The house, the business, the cars.' Her face was wooden.

'Jo, dear. I am so sorry–'

'Both us in a bit of a mess,' Joanna made the attempt at a smile. 'Oh – and just by the way – Adam has gone.'

'Now that is good news!' and Laura smiled.

'Thanks, Laura. You're such a friend.'

'Well, you know what I thought – but I'm sorry for you, just the same. He wasn't right for you, Jo.'

'Too young, you mean?' Joanna sounded cynical.

'No. Just not right.'

'Well, no matter now.'

'What are you going to do about the business – your mother, I mean?'

'Well, Ted – you remember Ted Layers, the manager? He has been wonderful, apparently – not only that, but he and Mother are an item, she tells me.'

'No!'

'He has asked her to marry him. Anyway, this is for the future. In the meantime, she has to sell the house, the receivers take over, the cars go – everything – I of course, have my cottage – and my car – that's yet to be sorted. They are mine.'

'And what will you do?' Laura was curious.

'Dunno. Something, that's for sure. I'm helping out at the showrooms – there's lots to do – and I'm quite handy with the book work and helping the visiting receivers.'

'Very depressing,' Laura said with a shudder.

'Yes, it is, but I'll live,' Joanna said. 'So will my mother. She's a survivor.'

'You're late,' Nell Dorgan said, looking up at the clock when Mandy came in. She was ironing one of her husband's shirts. 'I thought you were going to be finished at twelve today.'

'I was,' Mandy said taking off her gloves. 'But Milady,' and she stressed the word. 'Milady asked me to buy her some fish.' She took off her jacket and hung it on the door. '"My husband and I..."'

'Thinks she's the Queen,' Nell interrupted, ironing the collar.

'"...would like fish tonight, so Mandy, if you would go into Mr Garland's and buy two very nice Dover soles I would be very grateful. I don't know what the girls are having,"' she put on Julia Davenport's voice, '"the eternal pasta I expect – but make sure the soles are fresh, but then, Mr Garland always gives me special attention. He wouldn't dream of sending me anything that wasn't first rate." And she knew it was my early day.'

'Did you get them?'

'Yes, of course. He wouldn't let her ladyship down. You wouldn't believe it if you saw her. Lying there on that sofa – chaise something she calls it – in a blue lace dressing-gown–'

Nell frowned. 'Blue lace?'

'Well, no, not really lace, but it's silk, all edged with lace–'

'Housecoat, you mean.' Nell put the shirt on a wire hanger and hung it over the airer.

'No, not housecoat. It's more like an evening dress with long sleeves. Such a lovely colour. Sort of midnight blue – and you can imagine with that silver hair, and she wears high-heeled silver slippers–'

Nell frowned. 'What's she doing in that get-up in the morning?'

'She never gets dressed until lunchtime.'

Nell clucked. 'Some people...'

She folded the ironing board and put it in the cupboard under the stairs.

'Well, I've made us a sandwich – I thought we'd eat tonight when Dad's home, then we can go this afternoon to see that new film. Lay the table, there's a good girl.'

Mandy did as she was told.

'I tell you something,' Nell went on. 'I'm right worried about young Laura. I know she's got a lot on her plate at the moment, still–'

'She'll be all right, Mum. Once she gets

rid of the business – it's not her cup of tea, is it?'

'No, more's the pity, and he's not much use – thinks of nothing but his books and that – oh, it was a sad day when the old man died.'

'Well, he couldn't have gone on for ever, could he?'

'That's true,' Nell said. 'Now for the kettle – and get out the sandwiches; I made tuna fish and salad cream.'

'Lovely,' Mandy said.

They got on like a house on fire.

Chapter Four

Joanna arrived back at Saltwater Cottage around mid-morning, and somehow was not surprised to see Adam's car sitting outside in the drive. With beating heart, she let herself in, and saw him get to his feet where he had been sitting at the kitchen table, a newspaper in front of him and his overcoat over a chair.

Her instinct was to run to him – but one look at his face told her what misery he was going through.

'Joanna,' he said. 'I hope you don't mind, I let myself in.'

'So I see,' she said, her tone belying what was in her heart.

'I thought I'd take my things.' She looked down at the two packed cases. There certainly wasn't much luggage, because so little had actually belonged to him. His clothes, his personal belongings. She could hardly bear to see him standing there – he looked so young and vulnerable.

'I wouldn't have gone without saying goodbye,' he said.

'Thank you.' She sounded bitter but couldn't help it.

'I'm leaving McAllisters,' he said. 'I've given in my notice, and I – we're moving away.'

Did he know about the firm, she wondered. And what did it matter now? It was all water under the bridge.

She could hardly bear it, knowing how empty the house would be without him. But somehow she steeled herself, thinking of the trouble her mother was in, and what lay in front of her.

'Well,' she said. 'Goodbye, Adam–'

He came towards her, and she backed

away, thinking he might be going to kiss her. 'I'm sorry,' he said. 'I'm truly sorry, Joanna.'

She walked to the front door and opened it; he picked up his cases and his overcoat and walked to the car. She saw him, teeth clenched – he really did look dejected – and with a last-minute flash of sympathy for both him and the girl, she called out, 'Adam!' He looked startled. 'Good luck,' she said, and closed the door, standing with her back to it, and trying not to weep. Well, she thought, excusing herself, he really did make me very happy. Happier than I've ever been. At least I've had that.

The closing down of McAllisters was a shock to everyone, the worst part being the news for the employees, not only in the showroom, where they held well-paid jobs, but in the workshops, where the mechanics had been the finest available to the industry. What were the chances of them gaining employment in the future, with the market as it was, Linda McAllister wondered. Eventually the market would pick up again after a recession, it always did, but God knew how long it would last, she thought, dreading the task in front of her.

She found Joanna unexpectedly helpful. A boon – it was as if she submerged herself in the task to avoid thinking about her own personal troubles.

McAllister Lodge was put on the market, which upset them both, and the receivers who moved in informed them in no uncertain terms what would be theirs and what not.

'You said you saw it coming,' Joanna said. 'How far back was that?'

'A year or more. It starts when the orders get a bit thin on the ground, and gradually over the year you realise that business really is slacking off, and people aren't buying luxury goods like they used to. But you have to keep up your stock, mustn't be seen to be worried in any way.'

'I feel so sad for Daddy's cars – still, I suppose they were an indulgence. I remember so well those wonderful Concours d'Elegance they used to hold in Hyde Park and people brought their cars in absolute tip-top condition, opening the bonnets so you could see how immaculate they were inside, all gleaming and shining. But it will all come back, won't it?'

'Hopefully,' Linda said. 'We had a long run, after all.'

She stayed at the house until it was sold, and often Joanna kept her company.

Sometimes they spent the night at Saltwater and Linda would ask Joanna what she was going to do.

'Get a job, that's the first thing – when all this is finished.'

'Doing what?' Linda asked, sipping her coffee.

'No idea,' Joanna said. 'I'm not qualified for anything – spoiled little rich girl.'

'Now, now,' Linda said. 'You've got a good head on you. I've been really surprised how you've knuckled under, especially with these accounts and figures. You're almost as good as I am!'

'That's saying something,' and Joanna laughed. 'But I don't know that I could do it for a living.' She looked at her mother. 'What are you going to do?'

'Well,' Linda said slowly. 'Ted is going to open up a garage of his own – not prestigious cars – a repair garage – that's his line; and now is a good enough time as any to tell you that when this is all over we're moving up to Leamington Spa.'

Joanna's eyes were wide. 'Leamington Spa!'

'That's where Ted comes from and I wasn't born too far from there myself, so that's where we're going – but not,' she said hurriedly, 'before I know what you are going to do, and got you settled.'

'I'd like to earn some money,' Joanna said slowly. 'I've got the car and the cottage but they need keeping up–'

'Doing what?' Linda asked.

'That's the problem; I'm not qualified in any way. I thought perhaps a little shop – clothes?'

'Start up a business on your own?' Linda looked doubtful. 'That would be very difficult.'

'But there is one thing I'd like to do. When this is over and you've moved up to Leamington Spa,' and she frowned, 'will you really like that after London?'

'I've been lonely since your father died, and Ted is a great comfort to me. I don't want to grow into old age on my own. He's been very good to me – and I'd be happy with him.'

Joanna leaned forward and hugged her. 'Then that's great,' she said. 'I'm pleased for you. You've been a brick – Dad would be proud of you.'

'Go on!' Linda said. 'And what is it you'd like to do?'

'Take a holiday,' Joanna said. 'I've never travelled much, except to the West Indies on honeymoon, but I'd like to see a bit of the world – America perhaps, something like that – then I'll come back and settle down.'

'Good idea,' Linda said. 'Just don't rush into anything. Take your time.'

Three months later, the day that the McAllister Lodge contracts were exchanged, Joanna received a call from Laura. Would she go to dinner on Friday evening?

Joanna was delighted. She had seen very little of Laura since the bankruptcy had been announced. She thought Laura sounded excited. 'What news of the gallery?' she asked.

'Tell you all about it when I see you,' Laura said, and Joanna had to settle for that.

She took time over her dressing, choosing carefully; it was so long since she had been asked out to dinner, and knowing Laura's good taste knew that she would have to make the effort. She chose her narrow velvet trousers and a fitted black sweater sprinkled with jet beads. Black suited her. She put on her high-heeled shoes and the pearls her father had given her.

Linda was in the kitchen when she came

downstairs and Joanna knew that Ted would be coming round later.

'You look lovely,' Linda said, her heart almost stopping as she prayed, please make her happy again. She deserves a break. But, she told herself, she is young and resilient. She'll get by. 'Have a good evening,' she said, kissing her. 'And love to Laura – tell her I'll call in one day now that I'm more settled.'

'I will,' Joanna said, throwing a scarlet shawl around her shoulders, for the nights were drawing in. She got into her beloved Porsche and made for the High Street. She turned into Bridge Street then drove through high gates which were already open. The house was lit up and looked quite festive.

Laura opened the door in answer to her knock and Joanna saw that her blue eyes were positively sparkling. 'Joanna – it's great to see you – you look wonderful – come on in.'

She led the way into the beautiful drawing room, which overlooked the garden. Now, of course, it was too dark to see, winter was approaching; nevertheless the outside lights were on and the garden looked lovely with its evergreens and antique statuary.

Standing with his back to the fire was Simon, wearing a welcoming smile, and he came towards her, hand outstretched, and kissed her on both cheeks. 'Nice to see you, Joanna – it's been quite a time.'

His eyes always disconcerted her: intense eyes of darkest brown, which looked deeply into hers.

'Yes – I hear you have been busy on your new book – how is it going?'

'It's finished I'm thankful to say. The publishers seem to like it – that's the main thing.'

'Yes, I think champagne is the order of the day,' Laura dimpled, and pressed the bell.

Mrs Lawrence came in with a tray, smiling at Joanna.

'Hallo, Mrs Lawrence. Nice to see you again.'

'Miss Joanna – you look very well,' she said, with a trace of a Scottish accent. 'How is your mother?' Everyone by now knew of the failure of McAllister's.

'Bearing up,' Joanna said.

'Will you, Simon?' said Laura and handed him the bottle of champagne.

'Of course.' He dealt with the bottle expertly and poured out three glasses.

'Join us, Mrs Lawrence,' Joanna smiled.

'To the success of Simon's new book.' A fourth glass was poured and they drank a toast.

When she had gone, they sank into the comfortable chairs.

'Jo, I'm interested in what you are going to do,' Laura said. 'I know McAllister Lodge is under offer – but what now?'

'Well, as I think I told you, mother is going to marry again. They will be moving away – perhaps it is a good idea.'

'Did you know about that?' Laura asked curiously.

'No – well, you know me – wrapped up in my own affairs, I didn't notice what was going on. At all events, that's what is on the agenda. She is living with me at the cottage until they go – and well, until I get settled.'

'And you – what about you?'

'I shall get a job of some sort.'

Simon interposed at this point. 'What can you do, Joanna? Do you have any qualifications?'

'You must be joking!' Laura laughed.

'That isn't to say I can't get some,' Joanna replied. 'I'm not that dense. I thought I might take a business course.' She had thought of that on the spur of the moment.

'Oh, no! How boring!' Laura cried.

'Not necessarily,' Simon said. 'If you've never trained you can do a fairly quick comprehensive course which would enable you to get an office job. There are all sorts of things today, but you would need to know the basics – your father ran McAllister's, didn't he?'

Joanna made a face. 'Yes, until he died. And very successful it was, too.'

'Many excellent independent businesses are in the same boat unfortunately,' Simon said, and she thought how kind of him to say so. 'Do you know anything about the business?'

'Well, I suppose I must do. I was brought up with it.'

'She knows a lot about cars,' Laura interposed. 'She also,' she said impressively, 'has a Porsche.'

He whistled.

'I've had it since I was twenty-one,' Joanna said, 'and I'd like to hold on to it if I can. I couldn't bear to part with it but I will if the need arises. I'd rather sell the cottage first.'

'I'm sure,' Simon said. 'Couldn't you do something in that line, say a magazine – *The Motor*, *Auto*, writing articles, that sort of thing, on sports and prestigious cars?'

Joanna stared at him. 'I don't know. I've

never thought of it,' she replied. 'Hard for a woman to break into, though.'

'Why should it be?' he asked. 'You want to grab every opportunity you can – use your expertise.'

'Well – I don't have any except being around cars all my life–'

'So?' he said as if that answered the question.

'Anyway, enough about me. What are your plans? You'll keep the house on – Heronsgate?'

'Good Lord, yes!' It was Simon who answered. 'It's bad enough for Laura to see the business go without the beloved family home.'

'I'm glad,' Joanna said.

'That's the joy of writing – you can do it anywhere. I started in a bed-sit, and if I can do that I certainly can do it at Heronsgate.'

Laura took his hand. 'He's lovely, isn't he?'

'Yes – and so are you, Laura,' Joanna said. 'You take care of her – she's my best friend.'

'Oh, I will,' Simon said kissing Laura's hand.

'Another drink?'

'Tell me a little about the work you do, Simon,' Joanna said. 'Do the ideas come naturally to you? Do you enjoy it? You must do, or I suppose you wouldn't do it.'

'Well, it's a money-spinner if you get the right formula,' he said. 'I've been lucky, I suppose.'

'He's hoping to get a series on television, aren't you, darling?' Laura asked.

'Yes – fingers crossed,' he smiled. 'They liked my pilot story, so there's hope.'

'What's the basis of good thriller-writing?' Joanna asked. She was genuinely curious.

He thought for a moment. 'Well, I suppose pushing characters to their utmost limit – and seeing how they respond.'

It seemed an odd way to make a living, Joanna thought, but it took all sorts.

Laura made her announcement after dinner, as they sat in the drawing room over coffee. 'We are going off to the south of France,' she beamed. 'Simon promised me when the book was finished, didn't you, Si?'

'I did,' he said. 'We're off next week – seems a good time to go.'

No wonder Laura looked happy. There was nothing she liked more.

'We'll be back in time for Christmas,' Laura said, and hugged herself. 'Oh, you can't imagine how I am longing to see the dear old south of France again.' She looked at Joanna severely. 'And I want to hear that you have become a fully-fledged business woman when I get back.'

'I wish,' Joanna said and thought not for the first time how lucky Laura was to have captured Simon Woodward as a husband. He obviously adored her.

'Well!' she said, standing up. 'I must be going – will I see you before you go?'

'Probably not,' Laura said. 'And if not, take care – hope all goes well, and remember me to your ma.'

'I will,' Joanna said. 'Goodnight, Simon – have a wonderful time, both of you.'

'So,' Nell Dorgan said, a week later over a cup of tea. 'There we are then. Laura and Simon in France, the business sold – when I think of all that silver I've cleaned, and now it's all going. It's not even going to be an antique shop – it'll be a picture gallery.'

'Shouldn't think that will do anything,' Mandy said.

'Oh, I don't know. They say modern art is very fashionable at the moment.'

'It's hard to believe people can still find the money for that these days. Makes you think,' Mandy said.

'Still, I'll go in one morning a week just to help Mrs Lawrence with the heavy.'

'Mum, it's time you had a break, you don't have to do it.'

'No, but I like my morning out; it's the only one I have left, and she can do with the help.'

'Well – you're getting on a bit yourself.'

'Don't be cheeky, young Mandy.' It was all *badinage*.

'Oh, I meant to tell you, Louise Davenport has got herself engaged.'

'Oh, there'll soon be another wedding then.'

'Yes, January, they said, and you should just see the fuss Milady is making over it. What she's not going to buy for the wedding – trips to London, although how she'll manage it in her state of health, I can't imagine.'

'What's wrong now?' Nell asked.

'Where shall I begin? Her back, her legs, her heart, her nerves, she's exhausted.'

'But not too exhausted to get out and buy herself some clothes, I'll bet.'

'You're right there,' said Mandy.

Chapter Five

Joanna enrolled for a three-month business course, and although it did nothing to encourage her to take up an office job, nevertheless she was pleased that she had done it. She had gained confidence and knew that it would stand her in good stead.

By now, her mother had moved up to Leamington Spa with Ted and seemed to have settled down nicely.

Joanna found a job at the local doctor's surgery as receptionist, sharing the job with three other women, who staggered their hours in order to look after their children. She loved the work and was surprised at the satisfaction it gave her, feeling she was doing something worthwhile as well as keeping her occupied. The job would last three months until one of the young mothers returned to take up her old position.

In the meantime, Joanna had to think about her car; taking it back and forth to the surgery was not a good idea. It was not the most appropriate car in the world to be seen by patients and staff, and besides, she decided the time had come to replace it.

Enlisting the help of Jim Baker, who had been her father's right-hand man and who knew the car industry backwards, she knew she could leave it to him to get a good price. The fact that it had had one owner-driver helped, and they found a buyer immediately. Joanna also asked Jim to find her a small runabout that would be economical on petrol and cheap to run.

In the meantime, she rescued her old bicycle from the garage, cleaned it up and rode the mile to and from the surgery every day, feeling fitter and in better health than she had for a long time.

She was working on the day the new owner came to collect the car, and rode home, dreading the sight of the empty garage; but she put the bicycle away, and closed the doors behind her, unlocking the front door and letting herself in. Once inside, she had a little weep, then poured a glass of red wine, and because she was feeling sentimental prayed that the new owner would love her beloved Porsche as much as she had.

At the beginning of December she had just taken delivery of her new car, when she had a call from Laura.

'Dying to see you,' Laura said. 'Come for lunch tomorrow.'

'Sorry, Laura,' Joanna said. 'I only get an hour. My half-day is Thursday, though–'

'What?' Laura asked.

'I'm working – got a job in a doctor's surgery – receptionist,' Joanna said, knowing this would cut no ice with Laura.

'You're joking,' Laura said.

'No, I'm serious. Is Thursday all right?'

'Yes, of course it is, but Simon will be in town at a meeting.'

'Twelve-thirty?' Joanna said.

'Sure. See you then–'

She drove herself home from the surgery, then in the evening took the car for a drive around the area. If felt very strange after the powerful red car, almost like a toy, but there was a certain fascination in driving it. It responded to her touch and had great manoeuvrability. She found herself dodging in and out of traffic and certainly parking was less of a problem.

When she arrived at Heronsgate the next day, Laura came out to greet her.

'What's that?'

'Replacement,' Joanna said shortly. 'Porsche had to go. Don't even talk about it.'

Laura hugged her. 'I won't,' she smiled, and they went inside.

Once in the house she felt immediately at home; nothing had changed. After the disruption at McAllister Lodge, she had felt the ground moving beneath her.

'Come on in,' Laura said. 'Oh, it is so good to see you.'

'And how was France?' Joanna asked.

'Heavenly – as usual.' Laura certainly looked radiant, suntanned and slim, as Joanna followed her into the kitchen.

'You look wonderful – such a tan.'

'Well, the weather was great – you know how it is. Let's have some wine, shall we?' She poured two glasses. 'You could have knocked me down with a feather when you said you were working at a doctor's surgery. Oh, Jo – is that the best you could do?'

'It's great, I enjoy it: lots of people coming and going–'

'And all with something wrong with them.'

Joanna laughed. 'Well, that's where you find you're being useful.'

'How is your mother?'

'Moved up to Leamington Spa with Ted. They've quite settled in. He runs a garage, and they live over it.'

Laura made a face. 'Quite a come-down

72

for her, Jo.'

'It's better than it sounds. Truly – I went up there, and they're happy – that's the main thing.'

'If you say so.'

'Well, our lives have changed – yours too,' Joanna said.

'That's true,' Laura said, sipping her wine. She looked out beyond the river where the trees rose up into the nearby Chilterns.

'I didn't want to come back,' she said.

Joanna laughed. 'You never do!'

Laura sighed. 'No, I suppose – anyway, the shop is sold, at the moment they are decorating it; so we shall see a display of modern art. I am very interested as to what the new owner will put in there – after all–'

There seemed to be a wistfulness about her today, Joanna thought.

'Are you really happy, Laura? No regrets?'

'No. Why should there be? Simon is wonderful. The only thing is – he is not keen on the south of France; doesn't like the sun and the heat; there is nothing he likes better than to get down to work. I suppose you'd say he is a workaholic.'

Over lunch, which they had in the kitchen, Laura asked Joanna what she was doing at Christmas.

'Going up to Leamington, I expect. It'll be their first Christmas up there and the first on my own, so I'm quite happy to do that.'

'You could come and spend it with us. We'd be really glad to have you.'

'Bless you, but no thanks, Laura. Won't it be strange after all that has happened this year? Doesn't bear to think about some of it.'

'You're right there,' Laura said. 'How about some coffee?'

Joanna left about three, with Laura waving from the steps. How pretty she is, Joanna thought, with that lovely, pale, golden hair and wearing a silver-grey outfit; and she felt herself an utter mess. I must take myself in hand, she decided, peering at herself in the car mirror.

'Don't break any speed records!' called Laura from the steps.

She would have her hair done – restyled perhaps, and buy a new jacket – well, something. It wasn't the same, Laura being married. It was always difficult as a single woman to crash in on married friends. But she had a new life now – they both had. It was time to think of Christmas presents and going up to see her mother. Of planning her holiday – something she really must get down to.

Joanna spent her Christmas with her mother and Ted, and enjoyed it for what it was. It all felt strange, certainly, but the flat over the garage was spacious and Linda had brought with her the few things that the receivers had allowed her. Ted had some furniture; they had had the floor carpeted, not liking the noisy wooden floor, so it was cosy and comfortable. When Linda went down with a severe cold, Joanna stayed on several days to look after her.

Feeling she had done all she could, she made her way back home during that strange period when the lull between Christmas and New Year seems filled with expectancy.

On her return home she found several Christmas cards which had arrived late, one of them from an aunt who lived in America, her father's elder sister, Aunt Marion. She had not seen her since she had come over with her husband for Joanna's marriage to Tony Hargreaves. She was now a widow and lived in Charleston, North Carolina, where her husband had been an architect.

Now, she wrote:

Linda has told me all the news and I understand you are thinking of coming to

America. I don't know what you particularly wanted to see, New York, I expect, or the Grand Canyon, everyone does – but why not come and stay with me for a while, a few days or as long as you like – come via New York – I should love to have you and you really would enjoy it, I am sure. Cold at the moment, but say early spring, March, April, May – after that it gets pretty hot in New York.

Anyway, dear, think about it – I would simply love to see you, it's been such a long time.

Have a very happy Christmas and a wonderful New Year.

Much love
Aunt Marion

Joanna read the card over and over. Oh, how wonderful! There was nothing she would like more. She had been dithering long enough about what she was going to do for her holiday. Now she had the answer. She would go to America, to New York then Charleston.

The travel agents planned it well. A flight to New York, a five days' stay, then because

Joanna wanted to see as much of the country as she could, by train to Charleston with a stopover in Washington overnight.

Busy as she was with her work at the surgery, the three months having been extended, her days were full. It was early March before she saw Laura again, when Laura drove over to Saltwater Cottage to see her one Saturday lunchtime. Having prepared a light meal, for she knew that Simon and Laura ate their main meal in the evening, she opened a bottle of white wine, decorated the table in the little sitting room, which served as a dining room, with narcissi from the garden, and stood back to admire her efforts. She so seldom entertained these days. When she answered the door, she had a shock: Laura, carrying pink tulips, looked thin and pale, and most definitely under the weather. There were dark rings under her eyes, and she looked almost dejected.

'Laura, darling, it's lovely to see you–' but Laura thrust the flowers at her, and fell into her arms. 'Oh, Joanna, I'm pregnant – and I feel awful!'

Joanna was momentarily lost for words, then she hugged Laura, 'Why, that's wonderful!'

Laura stared at her. 'Is it? Well, take it from

me, it isn't!'

Joanna laughed. 'Oh, Laura these are early days – you won't feel like this all the time.'

'How do you know?' Laura asked. 'Your experience at the surgery, is it? Have you ever been pregnant?'

Joanna regarded her seriously. 'You know I haven't – more's the pity,' and realised they had got off to a bad start. 'Anyway, come on in. I am so pleased to see you, I so seldom see anyone here, and it's great–'

Laura threw her coat on to a hall chair, and went into the sitting room, where she flopped into a chair. She did look grim, just the same, Joanna thought, and recalled that some women lost weight at first, and what would she be? It must be early days. 'Anyway,' she said brightly, 'I'm sorry you feel so awful, although there is no need to tell you how much I envy you.'

'Easy to talk,' Laura said, still disgruntled. 'Sorry, Joanna,' she said suddenly. 'I'll try and liven up – but I feel so sick, so nauseated most of the time – not just in the mornings.'

'How far–' Joanna began. She had learned quite a lot since working in the National Health surgery, although she realised that Laura would have a private doctor.

'About fourteen weeks, I think,' Laura said.

Joanna quickly calculated – as much as that – she must have conceived in France; something that would please her eventually.

Now that Laura's coat was off, Joanna could see the round protuberance that pushed out her skirt, but elsewhere she was thin: her arms, her neck; and she had lost all her suntan.

She gave Laura an intimate smile. 'I bet Simon is over the moon.'

'Yes,' Laura said shortly, 'But then, he doesn't have to have it, does he?'

'Oh, come on, Laura, this isn't like you!' Joanna said. 'I've just opened a bottle of wine – perhaps you shouldn't–'

'Why not?' Laura asked. 'We're celebrating, aren't we?'

It was early May when Joanna ventured forth, a time the travel agents and her aunt confirmed would, or should be pleasant. She felt a little uneasy, setting off on her own, for she had seen Laura only briefly in that time, mainly because she was working.

Driving home after seeing her, Joanna was not altogether pleased at the turn of events in Laura's life. But it was no good worrying;

things would sort themselves out.

A weekend or two in Leamington, and here it was, the third of May, and she was wildly excited. The travel agents had recommended that she travel to and from New York first class. It was well worth the extra, they told her, and as it was a special holiday and she was not a seasoned traveller she would appreciate the extra luxury.

Even Heathrow seemed to be exciting, travelling on her own. She went to the Ladies room and gave a last glance at herself in the mirror. She was pleased with her new hairdo. It was shorter, and suited her. The faint blusher on her cheeks that she had never needed before gave her skin a special luminosity, and the brown eyeshadow enhanced her eyes. She had read somewhere that the Italian beauties she much admired advised 'any colour on the eyes so long as it's brown'.

I suppose, she thought, if I were younger, I would wear no make-up at all. Still, she was pleased at her reflection, and, heart thumping with excitement, she boarded the great jetliner, and was shown to a comfortable seat. The man two seats away from her looked up and smiled briefly and went back to his paper.

The plane was by no means full, due, she supposed to the disaster last September, but passengers kept arriving and after some delay the plane was airborne.

As the coastline receded below them and they were way out with blue sky all around them, seatbelts were unbuckled and everyone relaxed. Pre-lunch drinks were served, then lunch followed by coffee, and the passengers, pleased that there were no signs of turbulence, dozed off or read, and it was then that Joanna noticed that the man who had acknowledged her was reading a book by Simon Woodward. She craned her neck slightly to see the title, and the man looked up and smiled, turning the book over.

'*Mountain of Shadows*,' he smiled. 'Do you know him?'

As she had thought, the man was American. She blushed slightly at her nosiness. 'Yes, I do,' she said.

'Good, isn't he?'

Joanna, who had never read one of Simon's books, nodded.

'He is very popular in America,' he said and held out his hand. 'Mark Drayton,' he said. 'From New York.'

Joanna took his hand. 'Joanna McAllister from England.' She was pleased that she had reverted to her maiden name after the divorce.

The seat next to Joanna was unoccupied, and glancing at it, then at her, he said, 'May I?'

'Please do,' Joanna said, and he took his seat beside her.

'Good flight,' he said. 'We're almost there,' glancing at his watch. 'He's made good time.'

Joanna smiled. 'I wouldn't know – this is my first visit.'

'Oh, wonderful. There can be nothing more exciting than seeing New York for the first time, although the best approach to it is from the river. Still, poor old battered city – it's not the same – nothing ever will be.'

'You've been in London?' Joanna asked him, stealing a look at him. He was forty-ish, tall, well built, a typical American, as she would call him, with that slightly tanned look so many Americans have. Blue eyes but dark hair, slightly auburn. Married, she supposed, but she was attracted to him, nevertheless; he was that sort of man.

'All over – this time up to Scotland, which I have to say, I loved.'

'Yes, it is beautiful – my father came from there.'

'Hence the name,' he said. 'McAllister... Do you know it is quite a famous name in the South – or was – part of America's history. There was a McAllister among the Pilgrim Fathers.'

'Really? I didn't know that,' Joanna said, inexplicably pleased. 'That's where I'm bound for, the South; I have an aunt living in Charleston; I'm going there after New York.'

'Oh, you will love it!' he said. 'It is one of the most beautiful places in America as well as being part of our history. I'm a Yankee myself, but I love the South. Are you staying in New York for a while?'

'Yes,' she said. 'At the Waldorf for five nights, then on to Washington by train and staying a night, then to Charleston.'

'Good planning,' he said. 'You'll like Washington – every English visitor does.'

'So you work in New York?' she asked. 'It must be exciting.'

'I'm in publishing,' he said. 'Keeps me on my toes. What do you do?'

He assumed then that she was a working lady, she thought.

'I'm not working at the moment,' she said, hating to admit that she worked as a doctor's receptionist. 'My father had a car business, so all my life I've been surrounded by cars, but now that he and the business have gone, and my husband – I've picked up the pieces and got a temporary job in a doctor's surgery.'

'Your husband died?'

'No,' she said shortly. 'I am divorced.'

'Me, too,' he said, but he looked sad when he said it.

The pilot announced that they would be landing soon.

'Look,' he said. 'Would you allow me to escort you through to customs and all that? And you will need a cab – if I can be of assistance–'

She was more than grateful. 'Thank you,' she said. 'That's very kind of you.'

She was more than pleased with his company as he led her through immigration, which seemed to take hours, and felt guilty at the time he was spending with her, but she remembered the Americans' innate good nature and kindness, and an hour or so later was sitting in a yellow taxi with the almost unknown American beside her.

The drab journey through the tunnel soon passed and when New York itself emerged Joanna gasped with pleasure. 'It's just as I imagined it, but even more so,' she laughed. There was an exhilaration about the city – and nothing, she realised not even the bombing, could keep that down. They were survivors, these New Yorkers, people from all over the world who came determined to make it a New World.

Outside the Waldorf, Mark got out and helped her while the porter took her luggage, insisting that he paid the bill for he was going on further to his office. Joanna thanked him profusely: she had been so lucky to find someone just at the time when she needed him. Saying goodbye, he asked her would she have dinner with him on one of the nights – whichever suited her.

Joanna thought the night before she left would be nice. By then she would have seen some of the city and be more settled.

'See you Thursday, then – I'll collect you here,' he said, 'and we'll go to the Park Plaza – no one should leave New York without going to the Park Plaza – unless,' he said hurriedly 'it is on your itinerary.'

'No,' she said. 'Thank you – Mark – for everything.'

'See you, Joanna,' he said, and got back into the cab.

Well, of course, New York was all that she

had expected it to be, and more. From Fifth Avenue to Gramercy Park, she did it all, walking almost all the time: the Public Library; Macy's Bergdorf Goodman, where she was shocked at the wonderful merchandise and the prices; Times Square and Broadway; the trip round the river; the food. She loved the food. Fresh salads, tender steaks; she made the most of it. By the end of five days she almost felt like a New Yorker, and could see why it was that people felt it was their town. If you loved it enough it belonged to you. It was nothing like Paris, that feminine city, or London – dear old London – yes, you could say London was a masculine city, or it had been.

With such thoughts, on the Thursday, she waited for Mark in the reception area, feeling instinctively that he would not care to find her waiting in the bar.

He was on time, looking as handsome as ever. That he approved of her, she could tell by the way he looked at her.

'You look wonderful,' he said. 'And I love your dress.'

She was pleased with it herself; it was new, bought in New York on the spur of the moment. It was in her favourite black and with it she wore her pale pink pashmina stole and her very high-heeled shoes. She was glad of those, because Mark was so tall, and she felt quite diminutive beside him.

The Park Plaza was all she expected it to be. They drove through Central Park on the way, although she had explored this on her travels, not listening to the other English residents in the hotel, who had warned her not to.

The lights were dim, the drinks superb, as was the dinner; there were dimmed lights and sweet music – this was the New York she had dreamed about for so long, and she knew she was half-falling in love with this man. This man she knew nothing about – a complete stranger, you might say.

Over coffee, he asked her when she would be leaving.

'Tomorrow,' she said. 'I catch a train to Charleston – via Washington.'

'Are you returning to New York before you go home, or flying back from Charleston?'

'Yes, in ten days' time I shall be back here – then home.'

He looked straight into her eyes. 'Would you have dinner with me at the Waldorf the night before you leave?' he asked.

She knew she would before she agreed.

'I'd like that,' she said.

He dropped her home, and when he left her, kissed her lightly on the cheek.

Later that night, she wondered what they had talked about, for talked they had. About this and that; she hadn't said why she had divorced Tony, just that they were unsuited, but he had obviously loved his wife. She had left him for another man six years before – and he was still sad about it. Always searching for someone to take her place, and up to now he never had.

Well, there could be no future for them, she decided. She was too committed to England – it was her home, and she suspected he was too much of an American. Still, they were friends, and she knew she would look forward to seeing him again when she returned from Charleston.

'Well,' Nell Dorgan said to her husband, who was sitting by the fire – had been, in fact, since he retired six months earlier, 'I can't get used to young Laura being pregnant – she'll always be little Laura Troubridge to me, after all, we've known her since she was a small girl...'

She didn't expect a reply, and didn't get one.

She was dusting now round the mantelpiece, pushing past him to remove the china ornaments. 'I passed by the old McAllister place yesterday – seems funny to have new people in there – not seen sight nor sound of anyone since they moved in.'

'Any more tea in that pot?'

'It'll be cold.' She clicked her tongue and went to fill the kettle. Him and his tea.

Suddenly the front door was pushed open and Mandy came in.

'All right, then, Mandy?'

Mandy took off her hat and coat and hung them up. She looked tired, giving a sigh as she did so.

'Any tea in the pot?'

'I'm making fresh,' Nell said.

'I'll have one,' her husband said.

'Course you will – if it's not beer it's tea–'

'They were all there today,' Mandy said, 'The girls came to lunch.'

'And how was the bride?'

'Ohmi God!' Mandy yawned. 'Just like her mother – airs and graces – they talked clothes all the time. How is Laura?'

'I think she's better than she was. She is having a miserable time though; she used to be so well, and strong as a horse, all that swimming and that–'

'She'll be glad to get it over and done with – when's it due?'

'August, I think she said.'

'Rather her than me – thanks, Mum, nothing like a cup of tea.'

'You're right there,' the old man said.

Chapter Six

Washington had been a delightful city and everything that Joanna had expected it to be. She had been over to the White House, enjoyed walking the wide streets and absorbing the atmosphere. But she was impatient now to get to Charleston; and as the train rattled on through even more exotic scenery, the Spanish moss covered the oak trees, and azaleas grew wild with here and there a startling group of poinsettias.

As the train sped on she closed her eyes. How had she come to be here? Recalling her early days, her indulgent childhood – where had it all gone wrong? She knew now that she had never been in love with Tony; she had been in love with a dream, his looks, the charisma that surrounded him, his background – she hadn't wanted her lifestyle to change. At the time she had not been aware of this, but perhaps Tony had discovered it, too. There was something missing in their marriage: it had all been too cut and dried. Poor Tony, one of life's misfits – drink had seemed to be the answer to his problems, and she had it in her heart now to bear with him and to hope that he had found health and happiness with someone else.

But Adam – well, he was different. She had loved Adam with all her heart, finding in him all that had been missing in her life with Tony. But he was too young. She could see it now. Could they have gone into old age together, would there have come a time when he lusted after younger women? She smiled to herself. Well, he had done just that – and she didn't entirely blame him. If she had had a child things might have been different. If – if – such a useless word.

The train's whistle pierced her eardrums, and she opened her eyes. Charleston station was approaching, a busy, bustling place, and she collected her luggage from the overhead rack and made for the door. She recognised her Aunt Marion in an instant, her hair now a pale fawn colour where hitherto she had been dark-haired, and of course, she looked older, but just as pretty. Her face lit up as she saw Joanna, and she hurried forward and clasped her in her arms.

'My dear! How wonderful that you're here!' Her eyes were full of tears. 'You haven't changed a bit!'

Joanna hugged her. 'Aunt Marion! It's so good to see you – so far from home–'

'And as unlike home as anywhere could be,' laughed Aunt Marion. 'I think you are in for a few surprises...'

She led the way out to the waiting car, and having stowed Joanna's luggage in the boot, drove through the city to the outskirts, talking all the time and giving her niece covert glances. As they cleared the busy commercial streets the bustle of a busy port slowed down and soon they were among some of the most beautiful streets of houses that Joanna had ever seen.

'Oh!' she gasped. 'Aunt Marion – it's beautiful – and the gardens and the churches!'

'I hope you will learn to love it as much as I do,' her aunt said, as she pointed out some of the famous streets.

'No wonder Uncle Ben wanted to live here: the architecture is simply beautiful, like nowhere else I've ever seen.'

'I live on Church Street, right down here,' Aunt Marion said. 'At one time, when we were first married, we lived on Meeting Street, which is rather special, but I'll show you that tomorrow.'

The house was tall and narrow, and inside furnished with such splendid elegance that to say Joanna was surprised was the understatement of the year. She had never expected anything quite so gracious: the floors were wooden with wide polished planks, covered with exquisite carpets; and the furniture, she supposed, was English Regency and colonial. One carpet she recognised as Aubusson was overlooked by an elaborately carved overmantel.

'Let me show you to your room,' Aunt Marion said. 'You must be tired after your long train journey.' Up a beautifully curved wide staircase to the next floor, where she was shown her room, as splendidly furnished as the rest of the house, with its small four-poster bed and typical American quilt.

'The bathroom is next door – I hope you will find everything there that you need – and after you have rested come down and we'll eat. There's just the two of us so we can take our time. I can't tell you how nice it is

93

to have you here.'

'Thank you,' Joanna said. 'It has quite taken my breath away. I wish Dad could have seen it.'

'Yes, sadly he never did – still, never mind. You're here and I want you to enjoy every minute of your stay. Come down when you are ready...'

Over breakfast the next morning, Aunt Marion wanted to hear all the news.

They were in the large bright kitchen, which overlooked a garden formally stocked with flowerbeds and paved areas.

'You must tell me all your news,' Aunt Marion said. 'I was so shocked when your father died – he was no age, was he? Our parents both lived into their eighties.'

'He worked very hard with the business,' Joanna said. 'It was his life, so you can imagine how we felt this year when it went into liquidation. Pleased that he wasn't around to see it.'

Aunt Marion poured more coffee, and looking at her, Joanna could see a glimpse of family likeness: her father's way of looking straight at you, the curve of her mouth, the way her hair grew.

'And now your mother has married again,'

she said, and sighed. 'Well, I can't say I blame her; it's a lonely life, a widow's, especially when you have had a happy marriage. What is her new husband like?'

'A very nice man. He was Dad's manager for many years, and now they've gone to live in Leamington Spa.'

'So, you miss her,' Aunt Marion said. 'I was very sorry to hear that McAllister Lodge had been sold. Your father built that himself.'

'There was no alternative,' Joanna said quickly. She was not going to have any criticism of her mother, even though she was sure Aunt Marion hadn't meant it like that.

'Well – and how about you? The last time I saw you was at your wedding to Tony – and a wonderful wedding it was, too.'

'Yes, it was,' Joanna said honestly. For it had been. Only afterwards did it appear a sham.

'It is the saddest thing, drink,' Aunt Marion said, and Joanna looked at her swiftly.

'Oh, yes, your mother wrote and told me. I don't blame you at all – it must be absolute hell being married to–'

'Tony was sick,' Joanna interpolated quickly. 'He needed special treatment for alcoholism. Now I look back and feel

95

sometimes I failed him.' How could someone like Aunt Marion possibly understand?

Aunt Marion reached out and touched her arm. 'My dear, you mustn't feel guilty about it. You have your own life to lead – you are still young, let's hope that is all in the past.' She smiled. 'What about boyfriends?'

Joanna found herself colouring. 'One or two – but I'm not in a hurry. I have a little job – a temporary one in a doctor's surgery.'

'Good for you,' Aunt Marion said. 'Nothing like keeping busy.'

'Now,' she got up. 'When we've cleared away, I'm going to take you on a short sightseeing tour. Would you like that?'

'Love to,' said Joanna, and helped to clear the dishes away.

Presently her aunt sat at the table with an illustrated book.

'Have a glance at that while I go upstairs and get ready,' she said. 'You'll understand more what you are looking at then.'

Joanna opened it at the first page, as her aunt went on.

'Did you know that Charleston was founded in 1670 as "Charles Towne",' her aunt said. 'It was the southernmost settlement in British North America. The British colonists left Gravesend, England in search of a dream, an Eden, and about one hundred and fifty of the colonists settled – the bank of the river they would call the Ashley. Then they made a colony, completed in 1680, on the site of the peninsula whose two rivers, the Cooper and the Ashley, flow together to form the Atlantic Ocean (or so the story goes). Each river takes its name from Antony Ashley Cooper, Earl of Shaftsbury, one of the Lords Proprietors of the Colony. Charles the Second gave his name to Carolina through his Latin name Carolus, and he gave the land itself to Shaftesbury and seven other gentlemen as a reward for their loyalty. I'm telling you this, dear, because your Uncle Ben was a direct descendant of one of those seven men.'

'Oh!' Joanna was impressed. Her aunt looked so proud.

'Isn't that wonderful?' Aunt Marion asked with a beaming smile.

'Incredible,' Joanna said.

'Now, enough of that, I'll tell you as we walk around – but you can always ask me anything you want to know. Charleston is steeped in history.'

It really was an amazing place: Meeting Street, Tradd Street and the Battery, where they sat by the sea wall overlooking where the two rivers met, while in the distance Fort Sumter could be seen.

'It was here,' Aunt Marion said, 'that the Confederates on James Island began firing on the Union-held Fort Sumter, starting the Civil War. I expect you will remember all these place names from Margaret Mitchell's *Gone with the Wind*. She used many of the place-names – Ashley – Rhett–'

Joanna was enchanted with everything she saw.

'Some of the most beautiful houses are on South Battery, and here at Santa Margherita President Roosevelt dined during his visit in 1902.' She took Joanna's arm. 'You mustn't mind me – I'm on the committee for the preservation of Charleston, and I frequently escort tourists around. Just tell me when you would like a break. We shall have lunch in a nice little restaurant – French food, I know you will love it – and this evening I have invited a few neighbours in; they are so looking forward to meeting you.'

The next day, Sunday, they went to church, to St Philip's Church; such a homely church, with its balcony. The church was full; everyone was so friendly. The days passed by so quickly with invitations from neighbours to come for coffee or dinner – the hospitality was overwhelming.

On her last evening, Aunt Marion looked sad.

'I wish you could stay longer,' she said. 'But you must come again, and tell your mother to come and visit, with her new husband. I would like to see her – we always got on so well. What about that friend of yours – you were very close, weren't you?'

'Laura?'

'Yes, that's her, pretty blonde girl – her father had a fabulous antiques shop.'

'He died last year,' Laura said. 'And Laura, I expect you heard, got married – Simon Woodward.'

Aunt Marion frowned. 'I know that name.'

'He writes thrillers,' Joanna said. 'His publishers are in New York, as a matter of fact I met a man on the plane coming over who publishes him. He says he is very popular over here.'

'Yes, I believe he is. I'm not that keen on thrillers myself, but I do know the name. And is Laura happy?

'The business has been sold – she had no interest in the antiques business.'

Aunt Marion looked sad. 'Oh, what a pity. I recall her father as a very charming man.'

'Yes, he was.'

'Well, my dear, you've seen a few changes in Buckham in the last couple of years.'

'Yes, sadly,' Joanna agreed. 'But Aunt Marion, I've had the most fantastic time over here; it was just what I needed, and I think Charleston is the most beautiful place I've ever seen.'

Aunt Marion blushed with pleasure. 'Well, I have to say I agree with you, but then I am biased. I've lived here all my married life.'

'How lucky can you be?' Joanna smiled.

She was driven to the station the following morning and was genuinely sorry to leave, but she had the feeling that this would not be her last visit.

It was a long train journey, and reflecting on the last few days, she realised that it had been just what she needed. A complete change. Away from everything, to be able to get things in perspective. Her mother was nicely settled now, she had Saltwater Cottage and her little car, she was free to make her own decisions. The thing was to try not to make mistakes – get carried away as she was wont to do. She would get herself a job. She found herself thinking about Mark Drayton and looking forward to seeing him again.

Would he get in touch with her as he had suggested? Dinner on her last night in New York? She found her heart stirring as she thought of him and hoped he would. It would be the perfect ending to a perfect holiday.

This time tomorrow she would be at the airport and this would all have seemed like a dream. Still, she had this evening to look forward to, and saw again the tall American with his friendly eyes, his concern for her comfort.

The scenery changed and became more built-up as the train ploughed into the outskirts of New York and she sat back and closed her eyes...

There was a message awaiting her at the hotel in New York. A Mr Mark Drayton would be waiting for her in the foyer at 7 pm. She felt a rush of pleasure, and going to her room found a single pink rose in a small vase beautifully presented, as the Americans do. She smelled the rose – it was scented. A small gold card said, 'Please wear it – so I can recognise you – Mark.'

She laughed out loud as she ran the bath, then a thought struck her. What did he expect of her? More than she was at the moment prepared to give?

She put a toe in the soft, hot water. Symbolic, she wondered?

Her packing done, she looked at her reflection in the long mirror, and thought she looked a lot better for the break in Charleston. Relaxed, as if she was ready to face anything. She had the feeling that she might have looked apprehensive when she arrived, which may have accounted for Mark taking pity on her.

Well, it had only needed a few days, and she felt fine. She wore the black dress again, but pinned the rose to her shoulder – a corsage, she thought, you never hear that word used now, and thought how nice it looked. So he was a romantic, which was nice. She liked that in a man. Adam had been but not Tony. Tony was far too macho – he would have found it a sign of weakness. A last glimpse in the mirror, and she made her way to the lift.

Mark was waiting for her in the lobby and she knew by his expression that he was pleased and liked what he saw. He smiled at her, taking in her small, slim figure, her glossy hair.

'Welcome back,' he said. 'You look as if

you had a wonderful trip.'

'I did,' Joanna said. 'It really was an experience – so beautiful I hardly wanted to leave. Still, I shall be back.'

'I am very glad to hear it,' he said. 'Let's go into the bar, and you can tell me all about it.'

Over Martinis they sat and talked. The strange thing was Joanna felt she had known him forever, rather than a few days. He was so easy to talk to.

The more they talked, the more she learned about him. He was thirty-nine – a dangerous age, he said with a smile – and his marriage had lasted eight years before his wife left him to go on an expedition to South America. She had always been keen on the old Indian religions in South America and had met someone with the same interests at her evening classes.

'It was a passion with her,' he said, 'and I couldn't help her at all, not having the slightest interest in any of that. I failed her, I suppose, but at least she has found someone to share her interest, and we just ended the marriage – just like that. Almost as if it had never been. What about yours?'

She told him as much and as little as she wanted him to know, not wanting to spend the evening reminiscing about Tony. She said he had been a sportsman, a rugger player who liked to drink too much and life became difficult. She mentioned nothing about being abused. That was her secret. And she didn't mention Adam.

They went into the dining room, and ordered. He certainly knew his wine, she thought, feeling quite exhilarated, for wine-drinking had not been one of Aunt Marion's particular things, and she felt more and more relaxed and had to warn herself to keep a clear head – it was so easy to get carried away. She felt almost as if she was floating on a cloud, with the food, the atmosphere, and when he took her hand across the table when the coffee arrived, she didn't take it away.

I suppose, she thought, the end result of this evening is fairly predictable, and after all, isn't a girl expected to pay for her supper? The idea of going to bed with him was certainly not abhorrent to her, and she felt like throwing caution to the winds. Why not? she thought, and knew that had she been really sober she would never have entertained the idea. That he would escort her to her room, afterwards, she knew, and felt, what a wonderful end to a wonderful holiday – although at the back of her mind a small Voice told her that she was not thinking with her usual cool common sense.

He seemed concerned for her – would she be all right on the plane going back – had she remembered all her tickets, her passport – was she packed...

They sat over coffee for a while, Joanna wanting to make the most of her last evening, and gradually sobering up as they did so.

Presently, apropos of nothing, she asked him: 'Did you finish the book?'

'The book?' he asked. 'Which book?'

'The book you were reading – Simon Woodward,' Joanna said.

'Oh, that – yes, I did. You read him too, don't you – he's great.'

'As a matter of fact I don't – but I do know him.'

'You know him?' He seemed surprised. 'Well, what about that? He's a nice guy, isn't he? I've met him several times.'

'He is married to an old friend of mine,' Joanna said and suddenly he looked serious.

'Really? Well, I guess he must be really concerned about her.'

Joanna was suddenly very sober. Concerned about her? 'Who? What do you mean?'

'Well – his wife's gone missing.'

Joanna felt as though she had had cold water thrown in her face. 'Missing? Laura?'

'Yes. Laura Woodward.'

'How do you know?' she asked calmly.

'Got the news over the grapevine – I think it was in the English papers.'

'Oh, my God!' She was stunned.

'Gee – I'm sorry – I had no idea that you knew her.'

'She was – is – my best friend,' Joanna said. She pushed her chair away. 'Oh, Mark, excuse me. I have to go. I must make a phone call–'

'Sure,' he said. 'I'll come with you.'

'No – no, you don't have to.'

They were in the lift in no time, and once in the room, Joanna dialled Laura's number.

'Heronsgate,' a voice answered, which Joanna recognised as Mrs Lawrence's.

'Mrs Lawrence – it's Joanna – Joanna McAllister – I'm phoning from New York – is it true that Laura is missing?'

'I'm afraid so,' Mrs Lawrence said. 'She's been gone a week now.'

'But where can she be? Does anyone know?'

'No. Mr Woodward has put the police on to it.'

'Oh, how awful! Well, I'm flying back tomorrow night from New York, and I'll be round as soon as I get home. Will you ring my home if anything happens in the meantime? The number is there, Saltwater Cottage.'

'Yes, of course, Joanna. Take care.'

Joanna collapsed into the nearest chair, feeling as if all the life had gone out of her.

Mark was at her side in a moment, and it seemed the most natural thing in the world for his arms to go round her to comfort her.

She was so glad he was there.

Chapter Seven

The journey was almost over, and Joanna had spent the time going over her relationship with Simon Woodward now that he had married Laura. It was strange that she should be going to visit him without Laura being there – although she hoped for everyone's sake that she had turned up by now, and realised for the first time that Laura must have fled almost as soon as she herself had departed for the States.

Well, for whatever reason, the idea of Simon being left depressed her more than somewhat. Whatever her reaction had been when she first met him, she was over it now. Possibly the fact that he had chosen her own friend had something to do with it. She recalled feeling unwanted and diminished. But she had been through a disastrous marriage since then, and a love affair, which had been lovely while it lasted, but what a year it had been.

Arriving at Heathrow, she immediately telephoned her mother.

'Joanna darling, how are you?' Linda said. 'Is everything all right?'

'Yes, I've had a really wonderful time – but I'm calling about Laura. Is there any news of her?'

'No, nothing, as far as I know. I telephoned her husband and introduced myself, but he has heard nothing. Seemed to be very upset, poor man... What on earth do you suppose could have happened to her?'

'I can't imagine,' Joanna said. 'Look, I'll phone you later, but I'd like to get home – sort a few things out–'

'Of course you would. 'Bye, darling, take care. Let me know if you hear anything.'

'I will.'

She went to get her car in the long-term car park and was soon on her way. It seemed strange to be back – it certainly was another world – but her thoughts were with Laura and what could possibly have happened to her.

The M25 on this fine May day was blocked to capacity, and it seemed to take hours just to do a few yards. Idling in traffic, she tried to put some sense into the words 'gone missing'. How could a young pregnant woman disappear so completely?

Eventually she arrived in Buckham and made her way home. Pleased that the cottage was safe and not broken into, as it was in quite an isolated spot, she sorted through her post and checked to see that everything was all right. In the mail there was no letter from Laura, which she had hoped there might have been.

She made herself a pot of tea, forgetting that she had no milk – it was the wrong day for the milkman – and then telephoned Simon straight away.

Mrs Lawrence answered once again. 'Joanna, dear,' she said. 'How nice to hear your voice. Every time the phone goes I hope it's Laura – but so far no news.'

'What do you think could have happened?' Joanna asked.

'I have no idea,' Mrs Lawrence said. 'It's as much of a mystery to me as anyone. Mr Woodward is out, but he will be back around four.'

'Thanks, Mrs Lawrence. I'll call round then.'

She unpacked her small suitcase and put her things away, sparing a thought, as she hung the black dress, for Mark Drayton, who had been such a help in New York. Any thought of romance that might have been had been nipped in the bud by the news from England, but he had assured her that there was probably no more to it than a sudden wish on Laura's part to get away. Maybe, she had thought, but still, it was frightening all the same.

She felt an urgent need to get out of the house and do something, and glancing at her watch, saw that it was two-thirty. She would get out now and get some food-shopping before calling in at Heronsgate.

It was surprising how quickly you got back into your stride with a bit of shopping in an English supermarket, she thought, and putting her carrier bags in the car boot, left the car and made her way down the High Street, stopping at the art gallery which had been the Troubridges' old antiques shop.

Since she had been away, the shop had been renamed, and in gold lettering announced itself as the Buckham Art Gallery. A single picture sat in the large window space – a very modern painting, some eight feet by six – although what it depicted, Joanna couldn't tell. The colours were brilliant and eye-catching, and peering through the window she could see one or two people inside, and the dark red walls held a few paintings. Well, she had time to spare, and pushing the door open, she went inside. A tall, dark-haired young woman came towards her.

'Good afternoon – are you just browsing?'

'If I may,' Joanna smiled.

'Of course,' the girl said.

It seemed hard to reconcile this large gallery with the antiques business that the Troubridges had run. Then it had been filled with every kind of artefact, now, the wooden floor was highly polished so that it seemed miles bigger, and with the few paintings on the walls resembled a real museum of modern art. Glancing towards the end of the gallery, she could see a man sitting at a desk, and the strange thing was that he seemed a little familiar. As he looked up from his desk for a moment, she saw a handsome man, dark-haired and tanned, dressed formally in an immaculate business suit. Seeing her, he smiled and got up at once, coming towards her.

'Ms McAllister,' he said with a slight bow. 'We meet again. Gerard Townsend.'

Joanna was astonished. Here was the man who had bought McAllister Lodge; she remembered him coming to view the house with the agent.

She took the proffered hand. 'Mr Townsend,' she said. 'Somehow I didn't connect you with this – gallery.'

'Oh, you didn't know?' he smiled, and looked around. 'What do you think of it?'

'It's wonderful,' Joanna said. 'Very impressive. Not,' she added, 'that I know anything about modern art.'

'We would be happy to teach you,' he said. 'Feel free to come in anytime and look around – we pride ourselves that we have some very good artists, and judging so far by our sales, Buckham is very appreciative of our efforts.'

'I am glad,' Joanna said. 'You have obviously filled a gap.'

'I should be happy to send you an invitation to our cocktail party in June – I do hope you can come.'

'Thank you, that would be nice,' Joanna said. 'How are you settling in at McAllister Lodge?'

'Oh, very well. I love it – great atmosphere – you must have been very upset at leaving it.'

'Yes, I was born there, but well, circumstances alter, don't they, and it wasn't a very practical situation for my mother and myself. I'm glad you are happy there.'

He looked down at her with a very understanding smile.

'Well, I must be off, I only popped in–' Joanna said.

'Nice to see you, any time,' Gerard Townsend said, and Joanna took her leave, not quite sure whether he was a really charming man or a charmer...

Joanna made her way back to the car park, all her thoughts now on driving to Heronsgate. It was five to four when she arrived, and she took her time parking outside the house and looking at the garden, now in all its glory with tulips and wallflowers, the rockery leading down from the house cushioned with colour.

Simon must have seen her from the house because he came out and down the steps to greet her. She thought how different he looked from the last time she had seen him. Obviously he was worried about Laura, as well he might be – what an awful thing for her to have done – or had it really been a voluntary move?

'Joanna!' he held out his hand and greeted her, kissing her on both cheeks. 'My dear, I am so glad to see you.'

She thought how pale he looked, how stressed, not unnaturally. 'I had to come,' she said. 'You know I would have before but I was in the States – it was there that I heard about–'

'Laura,' he said quietly.

'And quite by accident,' Joanna said, as she followed him into the house. 'I was actually dining with your publisher – well, you know him, I think, Mark Drayton.'

'Good Lord, you've met him?' he seemed astonished.

'I met him on the plane going over – as a matter of fact he was reading one of your books – that got us talking. On my last night there we went out to dinner and it was he who told me about Laura – I couldn't believe it.'

He led her into the drawing room.

'Well, you can imagine how I feel,' he said.

'How was she before she left?' Joanna asked. 'She was not too well when I saw her.'

Simon rang the bell for Mrs Lawrence. 'I'm afraid she wasn't all that wonderful... She wasn't excited, thrilled about it, as I imagined she would be.'

'If you don't feel all that wonderful, it's difficult to be pleased; it must be very draining,' Joanna said.

A knock came at the door, then it opened. 'Could we have tea, please, Mrs Lawrence?' he asked her when she came in.

'Of course, Mr Woodward. Hallo, Joanna,' she said. 'Did you enjoy your trip?'

'Very much,' Joanna said. It was difficult to feel thrilled about her holiday when she was faced with this news.

As the door closed behind her, Joanna leaned forward. 'You told the police, right away?'

'No, not until the next day – I didn't know if she might have got some bee in her bonnet and was staying overnight somewhere, but I thought it was odd not to leave a note or a message. The next day I rang the police.'

'And what do they say?'

'I think they regard it as more of a domestic dispute, which it wasn't,' he added

115

hastily. 'Seemed to think it quite possible that she has gone off to think about things—' He turned to Joanna, his dark eyes almost angry. 'Does she do this sort of thing? I mean, is it typical of her? After all, you've known her a lot longer than I have.'

Joanna stared back at him. 'Good Lord, no, not so far as I am aware. You must remember we didn't live in each other's pockets in later years. We were at school together and afterwards we kept up the friendship.'

'I heard she had a Scottish boyfriend who was killed in a plane crash – is that true?'

'Yes, it is,' Joanna said. 'Why do you ask that now?'

'Oh, I just wondered if she had any feelings left for him, if she'd gone up to – Edinburgh, wasn't it? Where he was killed.'

Joanna frowned. 'I don't think that's very likely; that was all a very long time ago – I'm sure I would have known if that was the case, that she... And the police can offer you no help?'

'No – they say they are leaving no stone unturned, but I'm worried sick about her.'

'Of course you are,' Joanna pressed his hand. 'You know, if you asked me, I would say France was the most obvious place she would go.'

'I suggested that and they have the French police looking out for her, but I'm not very hopeful.'

'But then would she go and not tell you?' Joanna asked, genuinely puzzled. She was thoughtful. 'She does love France so – and I think she told me you were not keen.'

'That's true,' Simon said. 'It's just that it seems a cruel thing to do – if indeed she has just cleared off on her own. Add to that the fact that she is pregnant and not very well–'

Joanna took a deep breath. 'I know it's none of my business,' she said, 'but she is a dear friend – and I hope you are too. Had things been all right between you, before–'

'I've always thought that what went on between married couples was private, but in answer to your question, yes, things were all right. We were perfectly happy.'

'Have you looked through her personal papers – letters?'

'The police did – nothing there.'

'Telephone calls? Her doctor?'

He shook his head. 'It's a mystery – and very worrying.'

Joanna was more concerned than she liked to admit. They were assuming, of course, that she had gone off of her own accord, but what if something really bad had happened to her? If she had been kidnapped – abducted. Following her own thoughts, she said now: 'Well, at least you haven't had a ransom note.'

He looked at her sharply. 'Why do you say that?'

'No reason,' she said. 'Stranger things have happened,' and thought, Laura was worth a great deal of money.

'Have you contacted her relatives, per-haps–'

'Yes, the first thing I did; no one had seen her since the wedding.'

She looked at him, seeing the usual alert brown eyes dulled now, and put a hand on his arm. 'It will be all right, Simon,' she said. 'As I remember, Laura is a creature of impulse and very inclined to do her own thing.'

'In that case I would regard it as utter selfishness,' he said.

Joanna was left with the feeling that Laura's reason for going had better be good or he wouldn't easily forgive her. Joanna, knowing her better, knew that Laura would think nothing of doing exactly what she wanted to do, without thinking of the repercussions there might be.

They drank the tea that Mrs Lawrence brought in in silence, each busy with their own thoughts.

'Where did you stay in France on your honeymoon?'

'I've already enquired there,' he said. 'In an hotel quite near St Paul de Vence – she had known it before – she was very keen on painting and art, as you know...'

'Was she?' Joanna said slowly. 'I didn't know she was particularly interested.' For some reason she thought of the gallery and Gerard Townsend.

'The police took all those particulars,' he said. 'I sometimes wonder if they really bother in a case like this–'

'Oh, I am sure they do.' Joanna said.

'Domestic disputes,' said Simon miserably, and Joanna felt she wanted to hug him. It was her maternal instinct coming to the fore, she decided. She wanted to hug him, make it better...

She stood up suddenly.

'Well, I must go,' she said, 'I haven't unpacked yet.'

He looked at her, as if seeing her for the first time.

'Joanna, my dear, I haven't asked you how you got on in the States.'

'It was great,' she said, picking up her handbag. 'Plenty of time to talk about that.' She reached up and kissed him. 'Now don't worry, everything will turn out all right; she'll be back before you know it.'

And she wished she had the confidence of her words.

'Well, I don't know,' Nell Dorgan said, biting her lip. 'It's a proper mystery – I'm that worried about her. She's never done anything like this before.'

The old man was dozing. 'Mmmmm.'

"Course she wasn't feeling well, that I do know. That's what makes it so terrible. I mean pregnant and feeling sick all the time – good thing her father isn't alive, poor old man. Then, of course, that Simon Woodward is a bit – well odd – I mean, you never know with people, him with his mystery yarns and that. He must have a funny turn of mind, that's all I can say. Didn't seem natural to shut himself up in the study day after day writing that sort of stuff. Still, young Laura had been happy enough until the baby came along.' She decided she might as well talk to herself; the old man certainly wasn't listening. Mandy might know something when she got in.

She glanced up at the black marble clock on the mantelpiece with the gold face. She had grown up with that clock; it had been her mother's before her. Ten to two – Mandy was late, and at that moment the front door was pushed open and Mandy came in like a whirlwind. She was wide-eyed and breathless from running, and woke the old man.

'Whatever is it?' Nell Dorgan cried.

She collapsed against her mother.

'It's Sir Dennis! He's dead – he died of a heart attack this morning!'

'Oh my God!' Nell Dorgan said. 'Now, don't upset yourself, my love. I'll put the kettle on–'

Mandy stared in front of her.

'Well, it's a shock,' Nell Dorgan said. 'Whatever will her Ladyship do now?'

Her words sounded kind, but around her mouth was a little smirk.

'Now you sit there and take it easy. And tell us all about it,' she said to Mandy.

Chapter Eight

There were five large and beautiful black hats at the funeral of Sir Dennis Davenport. Seated at the back of the church as she was, Mandy Davis could not help but see them, and she wondered idly who they were. The church was crowded, as was to be expected for the funeral of such a famous and popular man. Struck down in his prime, so to speak, although his prime had been going on for some years now.

Mandy had wondered if she had a right to be there at all, as the Davenports' cleaning lady, or daily woman, whatever they called her kind today, but still, she had wanted to pay her respects. He was a lovely man.

Female relatives, could be, Mandy supposed, perhaps sisters, or wives of business tycoons. It was a very well-dressed funeral, as indeed it should be, him knowing all those important people, and that.

One of the hats turned slightly, and showed a perfect profile, a dangling earring, a lovely face ... and Mandy looked down at herself. Well, navy was the next best thing to black, and it was such a fine, hot summer's day – it seemed all wrong somehow to be sitting in church for a funeral.

You could have knocked her down with a feather when she had arrived last Wednesday morning and been told that Sir Dennis had died the night before, suddenly – a heart attack, the housekeeper Mrs Carey had told her. Well, it was a good way to go. Still, not very nice for them as were left behind. Not that she had much sympathy for Lady Davenport. Oh, she'd been pleased all right – like a cat with two tails. She'd had them calling her Milady in no time.

Ah, now here she was, Lady Davenport, and Mandy turned her head. Small, looking frail, though she wasn't, she was as tough as old boots, escorted on either side by a daughter. Lots of women in that family, she thought, and there they were, all little beauties – and not a boy amongst them.

Still, she looked nice. Neat, extremely pretty. A black and white print silk dress, small, becoming hat, a wisp of white hair curling beneath it. They'd been married a long time – she would be lost without him. Still, she'd survive. She was a survivor, that one. Mandy herself would never have stayed on, but she liked the family, the girls and the housekeeper, and the work was easy. Such a lovely house ... a bit like Howards End...

Funny thing, Mandy thought, today was her fiftieth birthday. Funny to be going to a funeral on your fiftieth birthday. Still ... when her husband died she had been only thirty-six, and she had carried on working at the supermarket, but when someone told her about working up at Davenport House (Mrs Davenport had called it that) she applied and got the job. The hours were good and suited her, and the money she could do with – she had her widow's pension – and besides, she found the work quite pleasant.

As for him, he was a lovely man. So good-looking, tall, well built, very nice grey eyes he had, with a sort of twinkle in them – a nice nose, and his hair, grey now, or was, but still thick, grew to a point, a widow's peak, she thought they called it. And a mole just beneath his left eye, oh yes, he was a handsome man all right. And she – Lady Davenport – had held on to him; she had been lucky, but her rule was law. She ruled him they said, with a rod of iron.

Oh, now came the vicar, and the coffin carried by eight strong men, a polished coffin with brass handles that shone in the sun's rays coming through the stained-glass windows. On it, sprays of flowers – and Mandy swallowed hard. Oh, it was so sad...

And now the organ sounded, and they got to their feet.

The girl with the black hat and earrings bit her lip, and the tears sprang unbidden from very blue eyes. She was his private secretary. Twenty-nine years old, and she knew that life would never be the same again. No more trips to the States, those wonderful hotels, the intimacy of those luxurious bedrooms, New York, Los Angeles, Chicago...

She had been his mistress for five years, having started with the company when she was twenty-four, but it hadn't taken long. She adored him. Of course her family disapproved, but she had gone her own way. 'Old enough to be your father,' her mother had said in disgust, while her father just looked upset whenever she saw him. So she stopped going home.

Dennis had taught her so much, not only in a business way, but how to live life to the full. She had her own flat, paid for by Dennis; would she – did she dare wonder – had he made any provision for her? His death was so sudden. She wiped a surreptitious tear away with a linen handkerchief.

That could be a niece, Mandy thought.

Susan Leadbetter sat next to her husband. She was entirely in black, the large black hat pinned back off her face with a black rose. Her husband was, or had been, Dennis' best friend. Jack Leadbetter and Dennis Davenport had started out together as partners, and as the business grew and expanded, each had become very wealthy. Homes in the country and in London, a place in Italy – and in all that time, Jack had never suspected. She glanced at him now, seeing his face, his large square face, flushed now with genuine sadness, in his eyes a fear as to who would be next. Her lip curled slightly and she took a deep breath as he glanced at her, and she gave him a thin smile. He took her hand and pressed it gently then took up the hymn sheet as they rose to their feet.

Jack was a weak man, she thought. Sometimes, she had prayed that he might find out about her and Dennis, that it might bring at least some excitement to her marriage, but it had been left to Dennis to do that. God, what a man... And what would she do without him now? And that silly little woman who thought she knew all the answers, standing there, her daughters

126

beside her – and she breathed hard. Oh, Dennis, Dennis...

Mandy thought she recognised Mr Leadbetter – she had seen his picture in the papers – and that must be his wife next to him; she looked a hard-faced so and so.

Hilary Denning stood up slowly, her firm, sturdy legs encased in their black opaque tights, her feet in flat shoes. She had worn a hat, partly to shield her face, and because she hoped no one would recognise her; but never had she felt so ridiculous. Ladies golfing champion, all those wonderful week-ends over now, Gleneagles, the Scottish weekends; she must have been mad to come. Dennis was the only man she had ever really loved. She had never seen his wife before, let alone his family – what a shower... She hadn't imagined her like that. And those girls, his daughters – somehow she had never really thought about his family. When she and Dennis were together, rarely enough, they had enjoyed every moment. His family had never really entered into the scheme of things – but here they were in the flesh, so to speak... Well, she just had to pay her respects and she would be off and away, together with this blasted hat which she couldn't wait to take off.

Fancy all these people, Mandy wondered. So many, the church was full; as the voices rang out, everyone seemed to put their heart and soul into it. When they sat down again, Mandy took another look at the woman in the large black hat some two rows in front of her. She seemed to be alone. So elegant, small and wearing a black silk suit. Hair upswept underneath her black hat, which was enormous. Pearl earrings – she must be about – what – sixty? She wasn't young.

Madeleine Dessart had come from Paris. Quite simply, to be with her lover of some fifteen years. Her perfect English lover. She had felt her heart break when she heard the news. And of course, there were others – but only one Dennis. How proud she was to be seen with him whenever he came to Paris. That wonderful brief holiday in the Seychelles, where he had ostensibly gone on business. Oh, but he was naughty! Naughty Dennis – but still, she was lucky. That unobtrusive little woman must be his wife; how had she held on to him?

He had been faithful to her in his fashion, and Madeleine smiled to herself. Well, over the years, however brief, she had been the one in his life who had consoled him, for what was obviously a very boring marriage.

Could Englishwomen be anything but boring, she asked herself? It took a Frenchwoman to understand a man.

Very elegant, Mandy thought; she didn't look English, somehow.

Gwen Harrison sat beneath her large black hat, quietly crying. She had come all the way from Nottingham, leaving her two little girls in the care of her mother. It was a long time ago that she had met Dennis Davenport, when he had come to Nottingham for a conference and needed a stenographer urgently and she had been freelancing then, working as a temp.

Oh, what a handsome man he was! She had fallen for him, hook, line and sinker. But he had been fair, told her that he was happily married, and had no wish to leave his wife, yet she had practically thrown her bonnet over the windmill.

She hadn't cared. He had set her up in a little house, seeing her when he could, which lately was not often, but she had settled for that. Twin girls had been born six years before, and he had been more than generous. With her promise that she would never reveal their secret, she had been more than happy to settle for what she had. She lived comfortably, her two little girls'

129

education was provided for. Her mother had said, now that he was dead, perhaps she would find someone.

'No,' she had said firmly. There would be no one like Dennis. Not ever ... and her mother had sighed.

The eulogy was being read, and now it was over, they rose again to sing another hymn.

Afterwards, Mandy got ready to leave, and saw Lady Davenport bearing down the aisle, escorted by her daughters. All good-looking, as a family. She wondered how she would manage. Would she give up the house? Would Mandy still be required?

To avoid being seen, she looked down, at her plain navy skirt and jacket. Well, she had been a good-looking woman herself once. Someone had once said with those dark eyes she looked a bit like Norma Major. Still, she didn't want to catch Lady Davenport's eye. Perhaps she would disapprove of her coming. Well, blow that. 'Come on, Tom,' she said to the lad beside her, and smoothed his hair, which grew thickly and in a widow's peak. He had nice grey eyes, with that mole just beneath the left one adding a bit of interest. Yes, he was a nice-looking boy, the only male Davenport – and off to public school next year.

Oh, yes, she had a right to be here and to pay her respects, as Lady Davenport, her of the pretty face and petulant mouth, moved down the aisle with her pretty daughters.

Oh, what a successful man, she thought. All those people...

They crowded into the drawing room at Davenport House. Never had there been so many people present at the reading of a Will.

Many of them had received explanatory letters – not surprisingly, for Sir Dennis had been a very methodical man, and not the sort of man to leave knots untied or any room for doubt.

For of course, it was well known that Sir Dennis was very rich indeed. Millions, some said, but figures these days sometimes seemed mythical. The room was crowded, and Mr Prendergast, Sir Dennis' solicitor, and his assistant Bates, were very much in charge. Chairs had been brought in from every room, although Lady Davenport reclined rather than sat, pale as a lily, and never opening her eyes; it was such a foregone conclusion. She was flanked on either side by two pale-faced daughters.

Mandy was there, having been requested

to attend, and wished she could be anywhere but.

Having cleared his throat, you could have heard a pin drop as Mr Prendergast started reading. 'The last Will and testament of ... Dennis Thomas Davenport.'

Bequests to servants and employees; there were thousands of pounds involved; the list was endless; ten thousand pounds each to five hat ladies. Lady Davenport did open her eyes at that point and then narrowed them at these bequests – who were these women? But she tried to console herself: obviously secretaries past and present – he had been a very busy man. To his daughters large bequests. Lady Davenport had no fears until she heard the words: 'A bequest of five hundred thousand pounds to Mandy Davis née Dorgan, mother of my son, Thomas Jason Davenport' – and she opened her eyes wide, then fainted.

There was a general kerfuffle around Lady Davenport, and when the murmur had subsided, Mr Prendergast continued, '...Davenport House to be maintained and kept in trust for my son, Thomas Jason Davenport, until he reaches the age of twenty-one. All the contents of Davenport House and my house in Italy I bequeath to my widow, Julia Redmond Davenport, together with the residue...'

Having surfaced, the Davenports looked around for Mandy, but she had taken advantage of the lull, and fled.

'Oh, my God!' Nell Dorgan said when Mandy arrived home, white and shaking. 'Whatever did Her Ladyship say?'

Mandy shook her head. 'I didn't wait to find out. I just ran. But I've got a letter here–'

'Give it here,' Nell said, and tearing it open, began to read it, and read it through to the end.

'Half a million,' she said, 'and his school fees already paid.'

As the back door opened in came Tom, his face as open and honest as a twelve-year-old's should be.

'Hi, Mum, Gran, Grandpa,' he said, and flopped into the large cane chair by the fire.

'Hallo, there, son,' Grandpa Dorgan said. 'No football today, then?'

'Not today, Grandpa,' Tom said. 'Could I have my tea now, I'm starving.'

''Course you can,' and Nell Dorgan ruffled his hair.

He wasn't short of affection in that house.

Chapter Nine

Joanna couldn't concentrate on anything but Laura's disappearance. She cleaned the cottage half-heartedly, her mind totally on Laura, and in desperation finally telephoned Simon, who asked her round for a drink at lunchtime.

She felt sure in her own mind that Laura had gone to France for whatever reason. Why she had was something else that would eventually come to light.

Poor man – he looked so worried, and she wondered if the same thought had crossed his mind that something awful had happened to her. Well, of course it had, she told herself. It would be in anyone's mind when a person went missing. But it seemed the police were not taking it very seriously, and she wondered why.

She said as much when they settled in the study over a glass of white wine.

'They assure me they are doing everything they can – if she were a child it would be different, but a woman going off on her own and presumably in her right mind is not a rare problem. They did ask me if I would care to go on television and make a plea for her return, but I couldn't do that. For her sake – I am sure she is alive somewhere – I don't want it spread all over the tabloids.'

'But surely you feel you must do something – anything – in this situation. It was in the newspapers the first day, wasn't it? That's how Mark Drayton knew, I think.'

'I expressly asked for no newspaper coverage,' Simon said doggedly. 'And that's something else: I am due in New York on Friday for my new book-launch – I don't know though, maybe I shouldn't go.'

'Oh dear.' Joanna looked worried. It occurred to her to wonder if perhaps Simon was a cold fish – he could hardly contemplate going away in these circumstances.

'Join me in a sandwich,' he said. 'I'll get Mrs Lawrence to make some and we'll have them in the garden.'

'That would be nice.' Joanna was glad of something to do with her time.

When he had gone, she sat looking round the room, Giles Troubridge's old study, seeing the watercolours he had loved. She was pleased Laura hadn't got rid of all of them, and wondered why the memory of her visit to Gerard Townsend kept coming into her mind when she thought of Simon's remark that Laura had been keen on painting.

They had finished their lunch, when a call came through on Simon's mobile.

His face lit up as he listened, his eyes on Joanna's face. 'Well, that's something,' he said. 'It's nice to know the French police are on their toes. Thank you – please keep in touch.'

'They think there is a possibility that someone answering Laura's description got off a plane from London to Nice on the day she disappeared.'

'Well!' Joanna said. 'Although you wonder, don't you, how accurate they can be about a thing like that; after all, Laura in dark glasses – why would she have been noticed? Still, we must look on the bright side. As I say, I have always believed she has gone to France.'

She looked at him curiously. 'What are you going to do about your book-launch?'

'I have to be there by Friday – but I could be back Sunday evening.'

'I suppose you wouldn't want to miss it?'

'Not in normal times, but I hardly think I can be away, just in case anything happens.'

And neither should you, Joanna thought, but she didn't say it. She got up to go. 'I'll be off now; thanks for the lunch. You will let me know, won't you?'

'Of course,' he said, 'You'd be the first.'

As she drove away, she was more puzzled than ever. Laura would have had a reason for what she did, no question of that, even if it was on impulse.

She had so much to do herself: work out the rest of her life. She had had her holiday, and she thought briefly of Mark Drayton. You could depend on him in time of trouble. Somehow Simon Woodward didn't inspire confidence, and she couldn't think why.

In the High Street, she parked in the car park, and walked towards the shops. She drifted towards the gallery, knowing that was where she was heading for but not knowing why she was doing it. She glanced in the window. There was no one inside, and she pushed open the door. No sooner had she done so, than it came back to her. Almost without realising, her eyes were drawn to a small picture, in oils, and her heart gave a sudden leap. It was of a village street in the south of France, and she realised that subconsciously it had made an impression on her. She knew the village, it was called St Paulins; it centred round a tiny old church and straggled thence down a sandy path towards the sea. She had been there herself with Laura once, and remembered Laura splashing about in the sea, her lovely figure in a bikini. They must have been about sixteen or seventeen. She vaguely recalled a small house in the village which Laura's family had rented – what a time they had had.

She was lost in memory, starting when she heard footsteps behind her, and found Gerard Townsend at her side, arms folded, contemplating the picture she was looking at.

'Lovely, isn't it?' he asked.

'Yes, I've seen it before,' she said slowly. 'It brings back memories.'

'I am not surprised,' he said, smiling. 'It was part of Giles Troubridge's collection. I bought it from his daughter when he died.'

'Oh.' There seemed nothing else to say. You would have thought Laura would have wished to keep it, but then, did the place have any special significance for her? She couldn't remember if Laura had visited it again on her frequent and subsequent visits to France.

Did Laura know Gerard Townsend? She must have had dealings with him. She found it difficult to ask pointed questions and moved on.

'Do feel free to browse,' he said. 'We have a few others quite similar of the same place along here.'

'Thank you,' Joanna said, standing stock-still, and he walked back to his office. Further on, there were two more of the same place: one delightful study of the tree which grew alongside the little church and towered over it, and the archway that led to the great door, worm-eaten and pitted with age, being reputedly fourteenth century. The other one was of a row of cottages, with children playing in front of them, the blue sea forming a background.

Joanna thought hard, but her memory was vague. She peered forward to find a signature, but it wasn't easily visible, and for some reason she moved on, not wanting him to ask any questions. She needed to go home and think about it.

Back in the car, she wondered. Had Laura painted them? And if she was so fond of the place, why did she get rid of them?

Memories of their trips to France came back to her, most of which had been when they were younger, teenage girls, for the Troubridges had owned a small villa not far from Nice, although they didn't always use it. Sometimes they let it out – to Joanna and her parents on one occasion, but try as she would to remember, the visit to St Paulins was fairly vague.

She made herself a light supper, and drank a glass of red wine, She felt aimless after her trip to the States, at a loss. She couldn't quite understand Simon's attitude, either. Well, you had to live with a person to know them. Had that been the trouble with Laura?

She was reading a book in bed when the thought came to her. She would go to France. Why not? She was lucky enough to be able to go. She had no job, as yet, nothing to keep her here. She would telephone her mother in the morning. And of course let Simon know what she was doing. Would he be annoyed? Well, she couldn't help that. This was something she felt she had to do.

She began to plan.

Linda McAllister was pleased to hear from her, but surprised that she was setting off again after returning home so recently from America. 'It's Laura, isn't?' she asked.

'Yes, I must go. I have a feeling that's where

she is. The French police telephoned to say there might have been a sighting of her on the plane to Nice, but I'm not impressed with that. It's just a gut feeling I have.'

'Is Simon going with you?'

'Good Lord, no. I haven't even told him yet that I am going.'

'He might not approve,' Linda said.

'What I do with my life is my own affair,' Joanna said doggedly. 'I've known Laura since childhood – she is very dear to me, and I can't rest here. After all, I've nothing else particularly to do – why not?'

'Up to you, darling,' Linda said. 'But be careful – you've nothing really to go on, have you?'

'No,' Joanna admitted. 'Perhaps I've just got wanderlust after all this time; we'll see. I'll phone you again before I go.'

Simon Woodward was astonished when she told him of her plans.

'You can't really be sure that's where she has gone,' he said, irritably. 'After all, if I really thought that, I'd go myself.'

'Oh, no,' Joanna said swiftly. That was the last thing she wanted. 'You have important work to do, while I–'

'Yes,' he agreed, 'Where will you make for?'

'Nice, at first,' she said. 'To look around the Troubridge villa – I suppose they still have it?'

'As far as I know, but we didn't go there recently. We stayed at Moulimar, a small village near St Paul de Vence.'

'How do you spell it?' She wrote it down in her small notebook.

'Very efficient,' he smiled, but she had the impression that he was slightly irked.

'Could I have the address?'

'Why?'

'Well, if I'm going I might as well leave no stone unturned.'

He went to his desk and looked up some files. 'Here it is. When are you going?'

'Just as soon as I get a flight. No time like the present. I'll telephone you when I leave – will you go to New York?'

'I hardly think so, much as I would like to – I think I need to be around, just in case–'

'Sure,' Joanna said. 'Well, I'll be off.'

She booked her flight, having decided that it would take too long to drive there, although having the car would be a convenience. She would hire one. She made some phone calls, packed lightly, but remembered her driving licence, took her road map of that area of France and once again found herself at Heathrow awaiting a flight.

Nice Airport greeted her in blazing sunlight, which dazzled her eyes. Having dealt with the formalities, she took a taxi to a small hotel in the centre of Nice. Nice and convenient as a base, she thought, and booked herself in.

It was lovely to be in France again; the air was so scented, with the jacaranda trees and the bougainvillaea spilling over the walls – everywhere there were tubs of flowers, elegant, elderly ladies walking their poodles, young men and girls wearing the briefest of clothing. Oh, it was nice to be back – she could wish it was for any other reason but the one it was.

The hotel was comfortable and cool and after breakfast the next morning, having studied her maps, she made for the Troubridge villa on the outskirts of Nice. Her memory of its location was clear enough, and she remembered it well. The shutters were closed, the doors securely locked; there was obviously no one at home. She spoke to a neighbour, who said she hadn't seen the family all summer. She hadn't expected any more than that, and she walked back slowly to the Promenade des

Anglais, where she ordered the *plat du jour* and a glass of wine, and sat watching the passers-by: an enjoyable occupation in itself, there was so much to see. How incredible it would be if suddenly Laura appeared! She lingered on, enjoying the vista, and accepting the fact that she had given herself the almost impossible task of finding her, which could end in a wild goose chase. Later on, she would make her way to Moulimar where Laura and Simon had spent their honeymoon, knowing that to find any clues there was extremely unlikely, and she had no intention of getting in touch with the police if she could help it. This was to be a strictly private search.

The next day, she hired a car in Nice, and drove herself along the hilly road towards Moulimar. It was easy enough to find, and the hotel was in the centre of the village. She managed to get a room for a couple of nights, and after she had deposited her few things, explored the small village. It was market day, and there were stalls of every description, selling French bread, livestock, babies' and children's clothes, and the cheese and food stalls were mouth-watering. She had coffee, such excellent coffee, in a nearby café, and wandered around the town trying to see it through Laura and Simon's eyes. The road led down towards the sea, where there was a small inlet, obviously very popular with sunbathers and swimmers alike. The weather was very warm for June, and as yet the place was not crowded with holiday-makers. In her white shorts and T-shirt she didn't look at all out of place.

Back at the hotel, she rested on the bed, and contemplated the map. There was no sign of St Paulins; she would have to ask at the desk.

Having showered, she changed into a dress, and went downstairs in the early evening to order a glass of wine at the bar.

The proprietor, who also did bar service, smiled at her. 'Madame?'

How easy in France, thought Joanna, where everyone over thirty was Madame, no question of Miss or Ms as in England.

She ordered a glass of red wine, and took from her handbag a postcard-sized photograph of Laura and Simon at their wedding. For this, Laura had discarded her hat, and it was a very good picture of her.

When the proprietor put her glass on the counter, she showed it to him, and his face lit up. Thank heavens her French was good, Joanna thought. She spoke the language well, taking after her father, who had taught himself German, French and Italian in a very short time.

The proprietor obviously thought she was showing him the picture of Simon, and he beamed. 'Ah – M. Woodward!' he said. 'The writer – a charming gentleman! And his beautiful wife – they stayed here last year.'

'Yes, and they had a wonderful time,' Joanna said, finding it difficult to ask questions that would not arouse his suspicions. She had no intention of telling him that Laura was missing, as he might alert the French newspapers. She smiled back at him. 'She recommended this hotel to me,' she said. 'She promised to come back – has she been since then? I have been abroad recently.'

'No, sadly,' and he shrugged his shoulders. 'But I expect to see them back – perhaps later in the summer.'

He was about to excuse himself to serve another customer, but then Joanna took out her map. 'I was looking,' she began, 'for a place called St Paulins – is it far from here?'

'Ah, the artists' colony,' he said. 'No, Madame, just over two kilometres away. Turn right out of the hotel and keep going. Follow the sea; in fact, it is the next village along. Very small, very quiet.'

Once outside, Joanna hesitated as to whether to take the car or walk, and decided to take the car. Along an uneven road with the sea to her left, she passed a rocky terrain of low cliffs, before a few houses came into view, and the memory of it came flooding back to her. Yes, this was it, a tiny place, an extension of Moulimar really, but with a small church; and there was the tree and the row of fishermen's cottages – and she felt a *frisson* of excitement.

She pulled the car to a standstill some yards from the beach and sat looking out to sea. She remembered it all now, and the place hadn't changed a bit. She watched some small children playing on the sand, and in a nearby garden a small girl was playing with a puppy.

How peaceful it was; it hadn't changed at all over the years, but she imagined now was a quiet time. She left the car and locked it and walked down to the water's edge. She took off her sandals and paddled. The water was fresh and cold and she felt like a child again.

She lay down on the warm sand and closed her eyes. Just her sunglasses – they would have to do. She had forgotten to bring a hat, or suncreams, had never visualized lying on golden sands, feeling the sun seeping into her and warming her limbs.

Oh, Laura, Laura, she thought, I've come all this way, and for all I know you could be in South America. She thought of Simon, and Mark Drayton, of her dead father, and of McAllister's in full spate. What an awful pity it had gone. Her eyes closed and she drifted off into sleep...

She opened them against the sun, blinking, not sure if she had slept or not, to find a shadow beside her. It was a woman in dark glasses, a slim woman, very pregnant; and Joanna thought she must be dreaming.

'What are you doing here?'

It was Laura, and she didn't look at all pleased.

Nell Dorgan was trying to pacify Mandy, who was in tears. 'So tell me what happened,' she said putting the kettle on.

'Well, when I got to the agent's, he said he was very sorry, but someone else had pipped me to the apartment. He was very sorry, but these things sometimes happen.'

'That's illegal, isn't it?' Nell asked, who knew nothing at all about the buying and selling of houses.

'No,' Mandy was irritated. 'He'd seen it before me, anyway, but he came up with his offer and where I'd offered a bit less, he's offered the asking price.'

Nell frowned. It sounded complicated. 'But you would have paid what they asked,' she said.

'I know, Mum, but he got there first, and the solicitors are already drawing up the contract. Oh!' she wailed, 'it was a super flat – I wish you could have seen it.'

'Good thing I didn't, then,' Nell said, anxious to smooth over the difficulties. 'There'll be another one,' she consoled her.

'Not like that, there won't,' Mandy said. 'It was really special.'

'Who is he? Do you know?'

'What does it matter?' Mandy said. 'He's a widower – lost his wife a year ago, and he's moving out of a house into an apartment.'

'Well,' Nell began.

'I mean – what does he want a three-bedroomed, two-bathroom apartment for? He lives on his own!'

'Perhaps he's got a visiting family,' Nell said, anxious to appease. 'Oh, if you'd seen it! The river view, the large rooms, the fireplace – the agent said it was the best one in Dudley Court. There'll never be another

149

one like it, I know.'

'Now, you're just looking on the black side,' Nell said, making the tea. 'You see, sometimes these things are all for the best. They happen for a–'

Mandy blew her nose loudly, thus shutting out Nell's words.

'Here, have a nice cup of tea,' Nell said.

'Where's Dad?' Mandy asked.

'Taken Tom to watch football,' Nell said. 'They'll both enjoy that.'

'Well, I've got to find something soon, Mum,' Mandy grumbled. 'That would have been just perfect. Somewhere nice for Tom to bring his school friends, you know, a really nice setting, like he is entitled to, you know, Mum. I mean, next year–'

'I know, love,' Nell said. 'Have a scone and butter – I made them for Tom for his tea.'

'Lovely,' Mandy said.

Chapter Ten

Joanna jumped up, burst into tears, and threw her arms around Laura, or at least as near as she could get. Standing back, she saw that Laura's eyes were brimming.

'Bloody cheek!' Laura said, drying her eyes, but she smiled, as they looked at each other. 'How the devil did you find me?'

Joanna looked sheepish. 'Guesswork,' she said. 'Sort of.'

Laura looked down at the sand. 'If I sit down I'll never get up again,' she said. 'Is that your car over there?'

Joanna nodded.

'Let's sit in it,' she said, and they both walked over to it, Joanna holding Laura's arm. She couldn't be more pleased and excited. Whether Laura herself felt the same was another matter.

Once inside the car, Joanna opened the windows and they relaxed.

'Well!' Laura said. 'Never did I think – I still can't imagine what led you here.'

'Not such a long story,' Joanna said. 'I just

knew I had to find you – we were all worried.'

Laura frowned. 'Does Simon know you are here?'

'Yes, he knew I was coming to France.'

'Oh, God no!' Laura sounded in despair. 'He's not going to follow you!'

'Pity we don't smoke,' Joanna said. 'I could do with one right now – or a G. and T. – something. How are you, anyway? You look very well.'

'I was until you came,' Laura said.

'Can we start at the beginning?' Joanna asked. 'Tell me it's not my business, nothing to do with me, if you'd rather–'

'Well, it isn't, in that sense,' Laura said. 'Still, you've come all this way – you deserve an answer.'

'Thanks.' Having got used to the idea that Laura was alive and well, Joanna now felt annoyed and a little upset for Simon. 'Where are you living?' she asked. There were so few places around.

Laura pointed. 'Over there – the third cottage from the left – where the little girl is playing.'

Joanna screwed her eyes up against the sun. 'Why there?'

Laura took a deep breath. 'That's where

my lover lives.'

Joanna stared at her, mouth open. 'Lover?' she repeated. 'Your lover?'

'Yes, his name is Jacques.'

Joanna stared out to where the sea broke in little waves on the shore, ripple after ripple softly, gently. It was peaceful, nothing at all to do with this drama that was being enacted in front of her.

Laura was silent.

'Are you going to tell me?' Joanna asked. 'Don't if you'd rather not. But I think it only fair–'

'To Simon?

'To all concerned,' Joanna said. 'How long–'

'I first met him years ago – Jacques Bonnard,' Laura said. 'On one of our holidays – we're the same age – we fell in love. He potters about in boats, fishes – he'd be a nothing in our world,' and her mouth twisted. 'Anyway, Daddy thought he was not at all suitable for me to be playing around with – I think we were about nineteen, twenty... So we went home.

'When I was twenty-one I came on my own. Daddy thought I'd gone to Nice for a few days. Anyhow, I did stay in Nice, but I came over here. We still felt the same about each other. You might know by now, Jo, it's all I ever wanted: to be by the sea, lazing about, not having to dress up – it's my sort of life.

'Jacques asked me to marry him – well, I couldn't. I couldn't upset Daddy – Mummy had gone, I was all he had. But I promised to come back the following summer. We wrote to each other and sometimes telephoned, but I went in May of that year only to find he had got himself engaged to a local girl – Sylvie–'

She was silent for a long time, and Joanna didn't interrupt her.

'Well, that was that, as you might say. He said he would always love me, but well, I wasn't here and Sylvie was, and I was not prepared to throw in my lot with him. My father needed me.' She covered her face with her hands. 'It was a dreadful time. I went back to London, that's when I did my modelling course, and then the antiques bit. Anyway, the following year when we went to Nice, I came here and there she was. They were married and she was pregnant. The result is the little girl you see over there. Kiki – she's a darling.'

'But – the mother?' Joanna asked.

Laura had just got back from France,

Joanna remembered, when she was introduced to Simon. Had it been desperation that led her to marry him? He seemed eminently suitable... Caught on the rebound, you might say – but there had been no doubting Simon's feelings for her.

'Well, you know the rest, I married Simon. I thought it a good idea at the time, I didn't want to be alone, you see. I liked him – don't get me wrong, Jo – I didn't realise what an awful mistake I was making, what I was getting myself into.'

'What do you mean?'

'Well, I don't love him, and I suspect he doesn't love me. We are really ill-suited – but–'

'The baby?' Joanna asked.

'Oh, it's not his!' Laura said. 'Not Simon's.'

'Oh, Laura.'

'Well, I haven't told you, have I?' She bit her lip. 'Jacques wrote to me last summer and told me that his wife, Sylvie, was terminally ill. Their little girl was four years old – and I thought I must see him. I must...'

'Well, we came to France, and Simon came with me. We stayed in Nice, and it was not difficult for us to meet: Simon only wants to work, he takes his laptop everywhere. I would sneak out and well – only twice, but it was enough – I know it is Jacques' baby, well, I know. Simon is not all that bothered about sexual relations, in fact I sometimes wonder… He lives for his work, nothing else matters. Don't reproach me, Jo. I was desperately unhappy, although I tried. When the telephone call came–'

'What telephone call?'

'From Jacques, to say Sylvie had died. I simply had to leave, I dropped everything and flew – I had to be with him. I've been here ever since.'

Joanna digested all this slowly. 'It was a very cruel thing to do, Laura,' she said at length. 'Everyone was so worried. Couldn't you have said you were going to France? Anything to put Simon out of his misery.'

'Oh, he doesn't really care,' Laura said. 'How can I make you understand? He doesn't like being made to look a fool, I can see that, but he really isn't bothered about me. Truly, Jo.'

Joanna sat stunned. 'And this little girl–'

'I love her. And she will have a baby brother or sister.'

'Laura! How can you – what about home? Simon? Heronsgate?'

'I sometimes wonder if he married me to get a nice home. To settle, get on with his writing... I shall sell it. It's no use to me. I don't want it – you know me, Jo. I'm a born gypsy, really.'

'But you will have to come back and put things right. It's only fair. What will happen then? I suppose Simon will divorce you.'

'I really don't care what he does. I only know that I shall come and live over here with Jacques. The house, money, whatever – I'll give Simon a fair share.'

'I thought I was bad enough,' Joanna said slowly, 'but you're the cat's whiskers! You've been very selfish, Laura. Doing what you did to Simon – to everyone – we've been worried sick about you.'

Laura seemed quite astonished. 'You're not going to tell me he missed me,' she said, and her mouth twisted.

What an awful marriage it must have been, Joanna thought. And to think, if things had been different, she might have–

'I'd better go; they'll be wanting lunch,' Laura said.

'You'll have to come back, you know,' Joanna said. 'Even if it's only to sort things out. I am certainly not going back to tell Simon all that you've told me.'

'Look – let me think about it,' Laura said. 'Can you come over tomorrow? I'll meet you here.'

'Yes, in the morning. I'd like to fly back tomorrow – there's nothing to keep me here.'

She felt tired and dispirited, and disgusted with Laura. Sickened to think she could behave like this, to her husband, her friends.

'Around eleven, then,' Laura said. 'Would you like to come to the cottage and meet Jacques?'

'No – not at the moment,' Joanna said. 'I've a lot on my mind, and it's not a good time.'

'All right, then,' Laura said, and got out of the car. Joanna watched her for a little while, as she made her way across the sandy road, her slim figure carrying the extra weight of pregnancy, and she turned and waved as Joanna started up the car and drove away.

The next morning Joanna was up early, although she had slept badly, opening her eyes to what she realised was going to be a difficult day. She packed her few things, and after breakfast paid her bill and made her way slowly towards St Paulins.

Despite Laura's decision, Joanna had to prevail upon her to telephone Simon and tell him she was safe. How much she told him of the truth was her own affair. Joanna certainly wasn't going to discuss it with him.

Her own father would have said, never meddle in other people's private affairs. But it was different in this case; she had been genuinely worried for Laura's safety, never dreaming she was going to turn up such a hornets' nest as this.

Laura was sitting in a deckchair when she arrived at the same spot as yesterday. She turned a pale face towards Joanna, smiled, and got up slowly to join her in the car.

'We'll sit here, and talk, shall we?' She kissed Joanna briefly. 'What a mess!' she sighed.

'Well, it's of your own making,' Joanna said, having lost patience with her.

'Oh, I know I've behaved badly, but in my shoes you might have done the same.'

'Maybe,' Joanna said, 'Did you talk this over with – Jacques, is that his name?'

'He's a real person, Joanna,' Laura said. 'And I love him very much.'

'I'm sure you do – to have done what you've done,' Joanna said. 'And what have you decided?'

'I can't come back – I can't, Jo. Not until after the baby is born. Honestly, I couldn't face Simon. I've about eight weeks to go, and–'

'I can understand that,' Joanna said, 'but can you live with yourself?'

'Yes, I'm not sorry,' Laura said. 'I've decided that I'll phone Simon today.'

'Do you promise?' Joanna asked earnestly.

'Of course, if I say I will.'

Joanna wondered if she trusted her any longer. 'Please, promise me, Laura. As an old friend. If you do that then I won't have to face him and tell him that I found you and so on and so on – I couldn't bear it. It will be bad enough him hearing it from you, but to have me tell it – I just couldn't.'

Laura put a hand over Joanna's.

'No. I see I've put you in a very awkward position. Still, I didn't ask you to come.'

'Fair enough,' Joanna said.

'So what's the plan?'

'I'll telephone him, and tell him where I am, that I have no intention of returning to Heronsgate until after the baby is born, then I will – but not to stay. I shall come back to live in France – sell the house.'

'What about Mrs Lawrence? She's been with you donkey's years, hasn't she?'

'She can stay until the house is sold and I shall pension her off. I don't intend to sell until after the baby is born, so she'll have two or three months – you'll explain, won't you, Jo?'

'No, I won't,' Joanna said stolidly. 'You can do your own explaining. And I don't want to face Simon.'

'I promise,' Laura said. 'I shall ring him immediately and if he is not there then at his flat in town. I'll phone all around until I get him and I will explain – truly. That I'm not coming back – certainly not to him. Not ever.'

They sat silently for a few minutes.

'Well,' Joanna said. 'It's your decision.' And that seemed to be the final word.

'I can't see the point of hanging around.' Joanna turned to face Laura. 'I wish you all the best with the baby. I suppose you could say you've made your bed–'

'Quite literally,' grinned Laura. 'Believe me, I'm as happy as Larry here with Jacques. We should have been together in the first place. I wish you could have met him, Jo.'

'Some other time, when all this has blown over. I'll get going now; I've got to return the car and sort the flight out, so–' She turned to Laura, kissed her on both cheeks and gave her a brief hug. There were tears in

Laura's eyes.

'Thanks for everything,' she said. 'I'm an utter pig, aren't I?'

'Yes, you are; but let me know when the baby is born. You will, won't you?'

'Of course I will,' Laura said, and got out of the car and stood waving until Joanna disappeared over the sand dunes.

Sitting back on the plane journey, Joanna reflected on all that had happened since her arrival in France. Never could she have imagined such a scenario.

The most extraordinary thing was having to realise that however well you thought you knew a person, you really didn't. There were hidden facets to everyone's character, and who knew how they would behave in unusual circumstances? She had believed that Laura was in France, but never for that particular reason. A secret lover? All that time? It was almost unbelievable.

And then Laura's description of her life with Simon. Joanna was prepared to believe her, but then Laura had treated him very badly. All she could hope was that Laura would keep her promise and telephone him and explain. The thought of Simon ringing her and asking her how she'd got on was more than she could tackle.

She was home by eight-thirty, glad to be back, and she poured herself some wine and made a small snack. She didn't feel like eating. Tomorrow she would phone her mother and put her in the picture, knowing she would be horrified. She had always liked Laura, although she thought she was somewhat spoiled; but she blamed it on an indulgent father and the fact that her mother had died when she was young.

It seemed uncannily quiet in the cottage. An early night and a book, Joanna told herself, but knew that she would probably lie awake for hours mulling over Laura's story.

She waited all morning for Simon's telephone call and by midday began to think that Laura had let her down and had not phoned him, getting quite rattled at the thought.

She put the washing machine on and tidied everywhere; she had no wish to ring her mother until she had heard from Simon. It was twelve-thirty when she heard the car draw up outside and knew it must be him – she had so few callers. Her heart began beating fast as the doorbell rang, and she went to answer it.

He looked drained, as white as a sheet, and her heart went out to him. Whatever his faults, he didn't deserve this. Without a word, he brushed past her, and she closed the door, and hurried behind him.

'In here,' she said, leading the way into the small sitting room.

He almost collapsed into a chair, then faced her, his large brown eyes accusing her. 'You didn't see fit to phone me?'

She tried to act casually to put him at his ease. 'It wasn't for me to ring you, Simon,' she said 'I thought it had to come from Laura herself. In fact, I refused to get in touch with you until she had told you.'

'Your dearest friend, is she? And you had no idea any of this was going on.' It was a statement of fact.

Joanna shook her head. 'It was as much of a shock to me as it is to you,' she said.

'Yet you thought she might be in France, and went to the right place to find her – odd that,' he spat out the words.

'I didn't know this person existed,' Joanna said, 'and you can believe me or not, just as you wish.'

She turned away from him, not wanting to look at that anguished face. Had he really loved Laura? Or was this a natural reaction to being dumped for another man? She had no way of knowing. She only felt that what Laura had done was monstrous, for whatever reason, and her pity was for Simon.

'How did you manage to – locate her? Was that just luck, too? You seemed to know where to go.' Still accusing her.

'Believe it or not, by a process of elimination. She wasn't in Nice, nor at Moulimar – then I remembered going once to this little village nearby – St Paulins.' She said nothing about the small painting in the new gallery.

'And by a stroke of luck, there she was. Well done, Joanna.'

He didn't believe her, obviously. He was still bitter, and she didn't blame him. He was furious with her as well as Laura.

'Would I have gone,' she asked gently, 'if I had known all about it?'

He looked at her then, and buried his face in his hands, and when he looked up stared straight out of the window. 'And now I have an erring wife with a baby which isn't mine. Well, sod her – she can go to hell for all I care. How does it feel to have a best friend who does this kind of thing?'

'I don't expect you to believe me, but I am

shocked, and disgusted at her behaviour. I should never have thought it possible.'

'I'm sure,' he said wearily and got up out of the chair. 'Well, I'll be off. I can't think straight at the moment. I'll be in touch.'

She opened the front door for him, not knowing what to say.

'Simon–'

He stood still.

'If there is anything I can do–'

'I think you've done enough,' he said, and got into his car. He drove away without looking back.

As if it was my fault, Joanna reflected. She went indoors to telephone her mother, who would say, as she always did, and whatever the cause: 'It's all for the best.'

Was it?

Chapter Eleven

Louise and Helen were sitting in Louise's old bedroom at Davenport House. 'Don't you want to know what he looks like?' Louise asked.

Helen didn't look up. 'You must be

joking,' she said.

'But he's our brother.'

'Half-brother – if indeed he is that,' Helen said coldly.

Louise was incredulous. 'You mean, you don't believe–'

'Do you seriously think that Daddy would – Daddy would have an – affair – with someone like – our cleaning lady? Come on, Louise, grow up.'

'But he wouldn't have left her all that money if he wasn't sure the boy was his, would he?'

'She was probably blackmailing him,' Helen said. 'I don't put it past her – I never trusted her.'

'Helen! We all liked Mandy, you know we did!'

'Well, she was no better than she should be. Poor Mummy, how do you think she must have felt, hearing that – in public!' and she burst into tears.

For once, Louise didn't go over to console her. Her mouth set stubbornly. 'Well, I believe it,' she said. 'Daddy was too much of a businessman to leave her all that money if it wasn't true.'

'You can believe what you like,' sobbed Helen.

'Anyway,' Louise said thoughtfully, 'Mummy hasn't mentioned it. It's as if she knows it's true – and I think it is. After all, she may have taken it up with Mr Prendergast, and he would explain. Perhaps there was a blood test – you know, all that sort of thing.'

'Oh, go away!' Helen almost shouted. 'You seem determined to believe it. I don't know how you can!'

Louise went out and closed the door behind her. She knew what she believed – that it was true – and somehow or another she was going to find out. Going into the study, she telephoned and asked for an appointment to see Mr Prendergast. His secretary said he would see her the following day. She and Helen had noticed that instead of their mother's usual fainting displays and alarming 'turns' she had been acting quite strangely: spending a lot of time in her room, and refusing to see anyone. The girls were quite worried at this state of affairs, being used to continuous histrionics in front of their father.

At eleven o'clock Louise presented herself at Mr Prendergast's office.

He gave her a quizzical look when she came in and stood to greet her, holding out his hand. 'Ah, Mrs Rivers,' he said. 'Do sit down.'

She wasted no time, drawing off her gloves. 'I expect you have some idea what I have come to see you about,' she said.

'No,' he said. 'But I am sure you will tell me, and I will try to be of assistance. Is it to do with the Will?'

'Sort of,' she said.

'I'm not sure that I can discuss—' he began.

'Mr Prendergast, you have been my father's solicitor for many years; you knew him quite well. It is, as you have probably guessed, about the bequest to Mandy – Mrs Davis – and the reference to her son. Is this true? Has she a son? And is he my father's child?'

'Mrs Rivers, I am sure you understand that I cannot discuss the Will – perhaps with your mother as the chief beneficiary—'

'Well,' she floundered, 'I mean off the record.'

He gave a small smile. 'Not something that we are allowed to do, I am afraid. Everything between a solicitor and his client is in strictest confidence. I can discuss your own legacy, and I can tell you that according to your father's testimony, Thomas Jason Davenport is his son – his only son.'

He was only confirming what she had already known in her heart, and she felt herself go pale, but there was a small feeling of excitement nevertheless.

'How old is the boy?' she asked.

'Almost twelve,' Mr Prendergast said.

'Where is he – could I see him – does he live with Mandy – Mrs Davis?'

'That I cannot tell you. I am not allowed to divulge information of this sort. If your mother would like to make an appointment to see me, I can give her more information, but I am afraid–'

'I understand,' Louise said, getting up. She was sure now, she had got what she wanted: confirmation that the boy existed. She would do some ferreting out of her own.

'Thank you, Mr Prendergast,' she said. 'You have been very kind.'

He stood up and saw her to the door. 'Good morning, Mrs Rivers.'

She sat in the car for some time, uncertain of her next move, but now she had embarked on her enquiry she would see it through. There was an element of excitement in it, too. Having acquired a half-brother, even in these circumstances, was more than interesting.

She started up the car. She knew where she was going: to Nell Dorgan's house, where she knew Mandy lived.

Hallam Road was a turning off the High Street, along a row of terraced Victorian villas. She knew the number – she had sometimes taken Mandy home in very bad weather.

Her heart was thumping wildly as she stopped outside No. 14, and, after walking up the little path, rang the bell.

Nell Dorgan answered, and when she saw who it was she took a step back, as if to ward off something unpleasant, but Louise was smiling, charming – and adamant. 'Mrs Dorgan, I'm Louise – Louise Rivers–'

'I know who you are,' Nell said. 'What do you want?'

'I wanted a word with Mandy, if I could–' she began.

'Mandy's not here – she – she's out for the day,' Nell said.

'Oh.' Louise looked disappointed.

For once, Nell was at a loss.

'I haven't come to cause trouble, Mrs Dorgan.' Louise said, and she looked so sincere that Nell took pity on her. After all, what a shock they had all had, that family. It couldn't have been easy.

'You better come in,' Nell said, and Louise stepped into the narrow little hall, and was led into the front room. It smelled of furniture polish and was somewhat cool as if it wasn't used much; which was true – they lived in the kitchen which was large and a family room – but it was furnished nicely with a three-piece suite and there was a large fern in the fireplace.

'Sit yourself down,' Nell said, doing the same herself. 'Now – what did you want to see Mandy about – not that I can't imagine–'

Louise knew she had to choose her words carefully. 'To be frank with you, Mrs Dorgan,' she said with her warm smile, 'I'm fascinated to think I have a brother – well, a half-brother.'

Nell looked at her. 'Yes, of course,' she said.

'And I am not going to pretend it was not an awful shock,' Louise said. 'To all of us – our family–' She leaned forward. 'How old is he – Tom? Is that what you call him?'

Nell Dorgan looked so proud. 'Nearly twelve,' she said. 'He's a lovely lad.'

'I'm sure,' Louise said, and suddenly her eyes filled with tears. She took out a hankie, and dabbed them.

'It's so sad really, isn't it?' she said. 'I mean,

172

what people do to each other. My mother, of course is devastated, but that's only natural. She hasn't spoken much, so I don't know what she's thinking – but I can imagine.'

She put her hankie away. 'Where does he go to school?' Louise asked.

'Stansford Gate,' Nell said proudly.

'Oh, that's wonderful,' Louise said.

'He's down for Eton,' Nell said. 'Of course, that was his father's doing.'

'I'm pleased,' Louise said, and she was. 'I suppose – I suppose you haven't got a photograph of him?'

Nell, having got herself into this mess by inviting the young woman in, was not quite sure what to do next. 'Well–' she began.

'Please,' Louise said.

Nell went into the other room and came back with a silver-framed photograph of Tom. He looked out at Louise with his frank and honest face, the living image of her father at the same age that she had seen in early photographs.

Louise sniffed and swallowed hard. 'Oh,' she said. 'He's lovely – so handsome – and between you and me, like my father – but don't tell anyone I said so.'

They seemed to share a secret between them.

'I'd better go.' Louise stood up. 'I don't want to make it difficult for you – no need to tell Mandy I've been – unless you want to. It will be our little secret. You didn't mind, did you?'

She walked to the door. 'Thank you, Mrs Dorgan,' she said. 'And Mum's the word – OK?'

She walked back to her car, and Nell bit her lip. Closing the door, she went back into the kitchen.

"Oo was that?' her husband asked, still sitting in his chair.

'Lady from the Women's Institute,' she said. 'Now for a nice cuppa–'

When Mandy came in at six she looked radiant.

Dressed in a well-cut black suit and wearing a white blouse, she looked every bit as smart as that young woman who had called this afternoon, and Nell was proud of her.

'How did you get on?' she asked.

'Well,' she said, 'It's not as nice as the other one – well, I knew it wouldn't be. It's at the other end of the house, the darker end. Smaller rooms, but I suppose that wouldn't matter. The fireplaces aren't as

174

nice. Anyway,' she went on. 'I've decided to take it – to buy it, I mean,' and she laughed at her mother.

'Cost you an arm and a leg, I'll bet,' Nell said.

'But I can afford it, Mum,' Mandy said. 'I must have somewhere nice for Tom when he comes home from Eton – and Dennis would be pleased, I know.'

'Fancy it all turning out like this,' Nell said, putting the kettle on and getting out the cups and saucers.

'Anyway, I'm worth it!' Mandy said, and they both laughed out loud.

'Seriously, Mum – I'm really pleased. Of course, I shall need some nice furniture – can't hardly take what I've got–'

'Of course you can't,' Nell said. 'It'll be nice to look around the shops for antique things–' and she wondered whether to say anything about Louise's visit.

I won't spoil her day, she thought. I'll tell her later.

On arriving home, Louise was met by Helen in the hall.

'Where have you been?' Helen asked. 'You shot off without a word.'

'Just into Buckham,' Louise said. 'The

atmosphere in this place is really depressing. How do you think Mum is doing? Has she said anything?'

'No – Mrs Carey took her tea into her room and said she was writing letters.'

'Really?' Louise said. 'That's interesting. Well, she's got to emerge sometime – she can't stay in there for ever. I wonder we haven't had to call the doctor before now.'

'You're very hard,' Helen said. 'You don't seem to realise what a shock she has had. Imagine–'

'I know, I know,' Louise said. She did feel contrite. How would she feel in the same situation?

'I'll go in and see her,' she said. 'Perhaps she'd like a drink – a G. and T. perhaps.'

She tapped on her mother's door, and presently, Julia Davenport called, 'Come in. Oh, it's you,' she said.

'Just wondered how you were,' Louise said, sitting down on one of the elegant Bergère chairs.

'How do you think I am?' Julia said. 'Shattered.'

She looked it. She wore no make-up and her eyes were ringed with blue shadows. Already she seemed thinner, and she hadn't been to the hairdresser.

'Would you like a gin and tonic – or a whisky?' Louise asked, already feeling like a rat after her visit to the Dorgans.

'Yes – I'll have a whisky. I don't know what Mrs Carey is cooking this evening, but I decided after dinner we should have a little talk. You and Helen, that is. I think it's time we cleared up a few things.'

Louise suddenly noticed that among all the silver accoutrements on the dressing table, the photographs of her father had gone. There were several of her mother, she always took a beautiful photograph, and many had been with him, but now they had gone. There were just three – one on the chest, one by the bed and one on the dressing table. All in heavy silver frames, taken of her mother when she was young and extremely beautiful, especially the one when she was presented at court.

Those must have been the days, Louise thought.

Her mother turned to her, and Louise was shocked. Those beautiful eyes were completely blank. No warmth in them, nothing. She'll never get over it, Louise thought, the shock, and she felt like weeping. It had been awful – her mother's whole way of life had been swept away, just like that. What courage she would need, and she felt like throwing herself at her mother's feet – and begging her forgiveness. For daring to do what she had done this afternoon.

But something stopped her. She wouldn't thank me for it, she thought. There is no warmth left in her – if indeed there ever was any. It was Daddy who gave us the love and attention we craved. I can do nothing for her, except go along with her wishes. She is not going to break down and suddenly become the mother we always wanted. She is as she is.

She stood up. 'Right. I'll get you a whisky, sort out the dinner, and tell Helen – we'll have a little confab this evening.'

Julia looked at her with what seemed dislike before she turned back to the dressing table.

'Yes, do that,' she said.

After dinner, when Mrs Carey had cleared away the dishes, Julia remained at the table. Dabbing her mouth delicately with her napkin, she put her elbows on the table and faced them.

'I am leaving this house,' she said.

'Mummy!' Helen cried. She got up and began to go over to her.

'Sit down,' her mother said. 'I have made

my decision – although it wasn't difficult,' she added drily. 'The decision was made for me.'

'Where – where will you go?' Helen asked, her lip trembling.

'To Italy – at first,' Julia said. 'As you are both aware, this house has been left in trust and therefore belongs to us. I have no further use for it, but you and your families may come and spend time here. The expenses will be paid and the staff, Mrs Carey and the gardener, kept on – everything as usual, but I will not be here. I shall go to the house in Italy and from there probably to France. I will keep in touch – you will know where I am.'

Why was she being so hard on them? Louise wondered. They had done nothing; it was as if she was cutting them all out, her family out of her life altogether. Perhaps this was just a temporary blip, something she would review again when time passed and the blow softened. There would be no point in arguing with her.

'You have your own lives,' Julia went on, 'and I have mine. If there is anything you would like – any furniture, anything at all from the house – please take it. The house will not belong to us in a few years so there is no point in keeping it.'

'Mummy – does that mean we will never see you?' Helen's eyes were bright and wide. Louise had to feel sorry for her; she had always been closer to her mother than she herself had.

'Of course you will,' she said, 'but I want to be alone to rebuild my life.'

'Oh, please think it over,' Helen pleaded. 'You shouldn't do anything hasty – it's too soon.'

Her mother turned cold eyes towards her.

'And what would you know?' she asked. Her eyes were like flint, her fine nostrils flared, her soft pouty mouth set in a grim line.

'When do you think you will be leaving?' Helen asked.

'As soon as I am ready, my dear,' she said coldly. As they watched her leave the room, Louise had tremendous pity for her. What a blow she had had – no woman could take that lying down. Yet perhaps they should be pleased that instead of falling apart she had garnered strength from somewhere to make her own decisions. That she was cutting herself off from everything that had to do with her husband was obvious. How bitter a blow it must have been. And a maid – a servant in their house – a cleaning lady – oh, she should never have gone to Mandy's house today; it was the act of a traitor. She was more sorry now than she thought she ever could be.

What a mess. Helen looked distraught. Louise went over and put an arm round her shoulder.

'Don't be upset, Hellie,' she said. 'It'll take her a long time to come round.'

'But in the meantime – what about us?' Helen said.

'We've got our lives, as she said. Let her pick up the pieces of hers – she'll get over it in time. Isn't that what they say?'

'It's not just Daddy's dying,' Helen said. 'It's the–'

'Yes, well,' Louise stopped her short. 'To be frank, I don't think she wants us around. She wants to grieve in peace.'

Helen nodded silently.

Louise sighed. What a helluva mess.

Chapter Twelve

Joanna felt a strong desire to get home to talk to her mother. She dreaded Simon calling on her again in his present frame of mind – and who could blame him for feeling as he did?

A quick telephone call to Leamington Spa, and she was assured of a warm welcome, and a desire for all the news.

The journey up to Leamington was fairly easy, and on the way half her mind was on the situation between Laura and Simon. To Jacques, whoever he was, she gave not a thought – perhaps because she had never met him. He had not yet taken shape. It was difficult to imagine Laura pregnant with his baby, when all along she had thought it Simon's. And what a disappointment for Simon; it was more than most men could take.

Her mother hugged her when she arrived, and Ted greeted her warmly when he came up for lunch. By the end of the afternoon she and Linda had mulled it over a dozen times.

'It was so – secretive,' Linda said at length. 'I wouldn't have thought Laura capable of all that deceit. She's spoiled, of course, but even so. And you were amazing – working all that out in your little head–'

'It wasn't difficult, once you were there,' Joanna said. 'And I know Laura so well–'

'But you weren't expecting that.'

'Not in a million years!' Joanna said.

Linda poured them each a glass of wine. 'It seems so awful to give up Heronsgate – that beautiful house, and all that Giles Troubridge had put into it. Obviously, it means nothing to her. And what about Simon?' she asked curiously. 'Will he fight her for part of it? After all, she's left him, and to have another man's child.'

'But it's Laura's house, and hers to do with as she pleases,' Joanna said.

'And then she will settle in France, presumably,' Linda said thoughtfully. 'You'll miss her, Joanna.'

'Yes – although, there have been so many changes in our lives; already she isn't the Laura I once knew – and I expect I've changed, too.'

'Yes – you've been through the mill a bit,' Linda said. 'Have you thought what you are going to do next?'

'Find a job – do something.' She turned to Linda. 'Mum – are you happy?'

Linda thought. 'Yes, I am. As happy as I will ever be without your father. But Ted is a good man. We get on well – which is more than your father and I ever did,' she laughed. 'We used to fight like mad sometimes – the attraction of opposites–'

'I don't remember that,' Joanna said. 'You always seemed so close.'

'That was for your benefit, I expect. But I loved him, and he loved me. And we were good in the business together.' She thought for a moment. 'Ted and I have a lot in common. He's a comfort to me, he's there and that's what I want. I like a man around the house.'

'Seems as if I've lost out, then,' Joanna said drily.

'You'll find someone – if you want to,' Linda said. 'They don't grow on trees, nice men, but if you find him, as the old song says, never let him go–' and they sang together.

'We're quite good, aren't we?'

'Pity we're too old to start a pop group,' Linda said.

Her mother was always good for a joke,

Joanna thought.

She arrived home on Sunday evening and there was post waiting there from Saturday, including a square thick envelope, which looked interesting.

It turned out to be an invitation to a drinks party – a formal opening of the new art gallery on the thirtieth of June.

She felt a glimmer of interest – she remembered now that Gerard Townsend had mentioned an opening party and hoped she would come. Yes, that she certainly would – her social dates were few and far between. Ten days' time – and she found herself looking forward to it.

She heard nothing from Simon during this time, and decided he was best left alone to cope with his problem. He had all the facts, it was up to him to decide what to do about it.

On the last day of June, she drove along to the town. It was a beautiful evening, the river sparkled below the houses, and the lanes were lined with blossoming trees and the scent of hawthorn filled the air. A few lilac trees were in bloom, and she thought as she always did at this time of the year what a beautiful place to live – in the English countryside, especially by a river.

She parked in the public car park; no need now to wonder if the car might be scratched or damaged by hooligans who had nothing better to do. Ethel, she thought, the car looks like an Ethel, and she walked across the car park and down the street to the gallery.

Through the windows she could see many people, all with drinks in their hands. There was a lot of talk going on, which she could hear as she pushed open the door. Gerard Townsend came forward to welcome her, hand outstretched.

She noticed then what nice grey eyes he had, yes, more grey than blue, but eyes that missed nothing.

'Ah – Joanna, isn't it?'

His friendliness was obvious, and she smiled. 'Gerard.'

'So glad you could come – ah–' as a girl appeared with a tray of smoked salmon and bits and bobs.

Joanna helped herself. He had obviously got caterers in – or had his wife done the honours? She realised that she knew nothing about this man.

He took her arm. 'I don't know who you know – more people than I do, I expect – but come and meet Jimmy and Martha

Henderson; they are old friends of mine.'

He introduced them. A delightful couple, she in a fringed skirt; Jimmy, fair, bearded, definitely from the artists' circle, Joanna decided.

'We hear that Gerard bought your house – that lovely house – McAllister Lodge – hence the name.'

'Yes, my father built it,' Joanna said. 'I was born there.'

'How awful to have to leave it,' Martha said, but it was said kindly. They were interrupted by more friends, and Joanna wandered around the room, looking at the paintings, particularly at the small paintings of St Paulins. It was so familiar now that she felt her heart turn over.

'You seem to be attracted to those French paintings,' a voice said behind her, and she half turned and smiled. It was Gerard. 'Are you interested?'

Ever the businessman, she thought.

'Not in buying. I recently visited there, and it is an astonishing likeness.'

'I'm sure,' he said. 'I wonder what you will think of this – my latest acquisition?' He led her towards the end of the gallery, where on an easel draped with a cloth was a painting some three feet by two.

'I am going to unveil it presently,' he said, 'and I am curious to know what you think of it.'

'Oh – I'm no expert–' Joanna said hurriedly, and wondered why he was so interested in her opinion. She had told him she knew virtually nothing about art – modern art, anyway.

He left her then, to join the others, and she wandered, talking to various people that she knew, most of them curious as to what she was doing these days, and was pleased to be able to say that she had been to the States and latterly to France.

Gerard seemed to be very popular, she thought; not surprisingly, he certainly had a pleasant manner.

Presently, he tapped on a table by the easel, and everyone was silent.

'Hope you'll like it,' he said whipping off the cloth, and Joanna gasped, her hand to her mouth, as she found herself facing part of the garden at McAllister Lodge. Despite herself her eyes filled with tears. 'Oh, it's beautiful,' she said out loud. For there was the willow tree beside the pond. Mauve and yellow irises grew there in abundance in the spring, but now the leaves had turned red and yellow and orange, and had floated down on to the water, which gleamed like glass. The depth of the painting was such that you felt you were there and wanted to continue walking down the path to the wrought-iron gates which led to the rose garden.

'Couldn't not paint a view like that,' he said in her ear. 'It is so beautiful.'

'Who is the artist?' Joanna asked, wondering at the same time how much it was. How she would love to buy it; but it would be very expensive, obviously, and she wondered if he thought she was immensely rich and could afford it.

'For my sins,' he said.

'You don't mean – you painted it?' she asked incredulously.

He frowned slightly. 'I'm an artist,' he said. 'Most of these are mine.'

'But–' Joanna began.

'Let me get you another glass of champagne – we'll celebrate the launch,' he said. She watched his retreating figure. It had never occurred to her that he was an artist. She imagined owners of art galleries sold other people's paintings.

'I wonder if there is something you might do for me,' he began. 'Except that if you are in a hurry–'

'Not at all,' Joanna said, wondering what he had to talk about.

'Later, then,' he said, and she wondered if he might be going to mention the price of the picture which she knew she could never afford.

As the guests moved away and out of the gallery, he came towards her. 'Do go into my office – we can talk there,' he said. 'That's if you–'

'Of course,' Joanna said, wondering what was coming next.

He rejoined her in about ten minutes, locking the gallery door and pulling down the blind. 'Another?' he asked, seeing her empty glass.

'I won't, thank you,' Joanna said, and he sat down opposite her.

'I hope you won't mind what I'm going to ask you,' he began, 'but I'll come straight to the point. Do you work?'

What an extraordinary question. She was almost relieved.

'Not at the moment,' she said. 'Although–'

'The thing is – I need someone to help out in the gallery.'

She felt a slight feeling of disappointment. 'Oh.'

'You see, Gwenda – she's the young

woman who has been working for me – is going abroad. Her husband has been moved, and she's going with him. You know, a gallery is a very personal thing – and I wondered–'

'But I know absolutely nothing about modern art,' Joanna said. 'I'm not sure–'

'Well, but you could learn – that is, if you want to–' he said. 'You have a pleasing personality – you are good with people–'

'But I'm not a saleswoman – I don't think I could do that.'

'I am sure you could,' he said. 'That is – if you want to. And you could always refer to me–'

'I'm still not sure; I suppose I could think about it,' she said, wondering if it might be a little boring – after all, a gallery was hardly full of people. It could be very quiet, and she felt she needed stimulation – like in the doctor's surgery.

'I had a gallery in town, in Cork Street,' he said. 'I'm an artist by profession, and my pictures sell, but nowadays I don't paint all the time – and, well, I wanted to get out of London. Somewhere in the country – so when I heard these premises were for sale, I thought they would be ideal. And again, finding a house nearby – it was just the ticket. Not buried, nor off the beaten track, and near enough to town to be–'

Joanna was becoming more impressed by the minute. The idea of working in Laura's old premises, which she knew so well, appealed to her. So did this man, who was being so open and honest with her. Dressed in formal clothes, he was handsome and pleasant, well mannered, and he had the hands of an artist, although she found it difficult to imagine him smothered in paint working in a studio.

'Well,' she said slowly. 'What would the work entail? I have to admit, I have to find something to keep me busy, and I'm not trained for anything. I took a short business course recently, which I think will be useful in the future, but it didn't take in selling modern art, at which I'd be useless.' And she gave him her appealing smile.

'Of course, the time factor may not appeal to you – I have no doubts about your dealing with purchasers, but if I said it would be three days a week, and one of them a Saturday, how would you feel about that?'

'Every Saturday?' she asked.

'Yes,' he said, looking down. 'I – er tend to get tied up at weekends, so I have to have someone on a Saturday. The other days could be Tuesday, Thursday, whatever you wish. I would work on the alternate days. An art gallery is hardly full of aspiring purchasers, so there is only one of us needed. Should, of course, we do a roaring trade, then I shall have to take on extra staff,' and he smiled.

Perhaps, she thought, he needs the weekends for painting. At all events, his suggestion was enough to get her interested, but she mustn't jump at it, be seen to be too eager.

'May I think about it?' she asked. 'I'll telephone you, shall I?'

She got to her feet. 'Well, that was a very nice little opening party,' she said, 'Thank you, and I do wish you well.'

She glanced once more at the painting on the easel before she left. 'It is absolutely wonderful,' she said, 'And just as I remember it.'

'I'm glad you like it,' he said, escorting her to the door. 'Thank you for coming.'

'I will let you know,' she said, and thoughtfully made her way back to the car park.

Once home, she undressed and went to bed. Lying awake, she thought of all the pros and cons of working in the art gallery.

After a time, she wondered why she was doing this, since it was perfectly obvious that she was going to take the job. Curiosity about Gerard Townsend was enough – the job she had no doubts about. Either she would like it, or she would hate it, in which case, she would leave. After all, it was only a stop-gap until something else turned up.

In the morning, she wrote him a letter saying she was prepared to take the job, and would be able to start in a week's time, thus giving her time to sort a few things out.

It was a fine summer morning, a day full of promise, and she thought she would drive down to the post office to post the letter.

In her white jeans and striped top, she got Ethel out of the garage and drove through scented lanes bright with birdsong – it was a good day to be alive. Driving towards the river, she saw McAllister Lodge outlined against the sky, and on an impulse when she came to the crossroads, turned towards it. She would drop the letter in – no point in going into the town – after all there was no collection on a Sunday. Then she would get back home and do some gardening. She found the work appealing to her; it was therapeutic. She had come to it late in life, because she had always had someone to do it for her, but now she loved the feel of earth through her fingers, the sight of plants pushing through the soil with their new growth, and she had an urge to cut back the straggly bushes round the front door.

Her heartbeat quickened as she approached McAllister Lodge – it was, of course, like coming home. But as she neared the drive, she saw a girl, with dark hair cut short, wearing blue jeans and a dark top, coming out of the house and going towards the garage. She stopped in her tracks. Somehow, she hadn't expected that. A young girl – twenty or so – where did she fit into Gerard's life. On a Sunday morning.

Her face flaming, she backed into the nearest available space, and drove back to Saltwater Cottage. No point in going into town – she would drop the letter into the gallery tomorrow. Plenty of time.

After putting Ethel away, she made herself some coffee and sat outside to drink it. After all, what on earth had it got to do with her? He was asking her to work in the gallery as a part-timer. Well, he could have a hundred women there for all she cared. She took her cup back indoors and went to find the secateurs. Nothing like work to keep you going. Still – was it his wife? Daughter?

None of her business.

As soon as she stepped outside the telephone rang. It was Simon – Simon Woodward.

She swallowed hard. 'Hi, Simon.'

He sounded contrite. 'Joanna – forgive me for not getting in touch before – but–'

She waited.

'I do apologise for the other day – I was over the top and quite out of order.'

She felt instant sympathy. 'Simon–'

'I wondered if you – would care to come round for a lunchtime drink – just ourselves–'

Her heart sank – to talk about Laura all over again... 'Well–'

'Of course, if you're busy–'

'No.' She was honest. 'I was just going to do some gardening – yes – I'll pop round just for a short time–'

He sounded relieved. 'Bless you,' he said. 'See you – thanks, Joanna.'

It seemed a house of sadness when she drove up to it. Not the house she remembered, with Laura swimming in the pool, old Giles Troubridge busy somewhere in his much beloved garden.

She rang the bell, and waited. When Simon came to the door she was quite shocked at his appearance and her heart went out to him. Impulsively she gave him a swift kiss, and took his arm.

He took a deep breath. 'If I didn't have my work, I don't know what I'd do.'

They went into the drawing room. The French windows were open and Simon led them outside.

'What will you have? There's everything here.'

'Glass of red would be nice,' she said.

He returned with the drinks on a tray and some small cheese biscuits.

'Good health,' she said, noticing the strain around his eyes, the frown which seemed to have become permanent.

'Well, what are your plans?' she asked brightly.

He held up his glass to the light before drinking. 'Well, the first thing is, Mrs Lawrence leaves in two weeks. No point, she says, in staying on. I guess Laura has been in touch with her about the monetary arrangements and so forth.'

'Have you heard from Laura?'

'No – nothing – have you?'

'Not since I was there.'

There was a silence. There seemed nothing further to say.

'I shall sue for divorce,' he said at length.

Joanna felt a shock in the pit of her stomach.

'Well?' he asked almost accusingly. 'What's the alternative?'

Joanna shook her head. She had no idea what to say.

He handed her the dish of biscuits. 'Seems I made the wrong choice,' he said and smiled bitterly.

'Did you have a choice?' she asked, could not help asking.

He looked straight at her, those deep brown eyes boring into hers.

'I think so,' he said.

'Well, you're young enough to start again – make a new life,' she said, and knew deep down that she would be no part of it. Wouldn't want to be. What she had felt for him had died a very long time ago.

'How's the book coming along?'

He brightened. 'Almost finished. It's kept me going – I think they'll like it; I hope so.'

'Good.'

'Once that's done I shall move back to town to the flat – nothing to keep me here.' Again, there seemed no answer to that.

It was the following Friday.

'Well, that's that, then,' Nell Dorgan said, taking off her outdoor shoes and putting on her slippers. 'My last day at Heronsgate. I shall miss it,' and she looked sad. 'No point in going in again – Mrs Lawrence goes next week – talk about the end of an era.'

She looked down at the table, then at her husband. 'You've not even cleared the dirty dishes away!' she said to him. 'You get lazier every day – I don't know,' and grumbling, she began clearing the table.

Then Mandy came in, and Nell's face lit up.

'Oh, there you are – how did you get on?'

Mandy looked very nice. She wore a black trouser suit and a black and white silk blouse; her hair had been cut short and she carried an expensive handbag.

'Oh, great,' she said. 'Signed on the dotted line. The solicitors were ever so nice – helpful – you know, I told them it was my first house purchase. I'll have the keys soon, then you can come and see it. Pity it's not number 1, still, it's the next best thing.'

Nell looked so proud. A woman of property, her daughter.

'When do you reckon you'll move in?'

'Any time after completion date,' Mandy said knowledgeably. 'I'm not going to rush it; there's plenty to do before that. Carpets, furniture and that–'

Nell was really excited until a thought struck her. What would she do without Mandy there? And little Tom? To be stuck with – and she glanced at her husband sitting in the chair by the fire, non-existent now and replaced by a vase of paper flowers – with him all day?

Chapter Thirteen

After the telephone conversation with Gerard, it was decided that Joanna would work on Tuesdays, Thursdays and Saturdays, although except for the Saturday, her working days would be flexible. Gerard suggested that she came in on the Monday of the following week so that he could give her an idea of her daily routine, which would start at ten and finish at five. His payment seemed generous enough, and Joanna was satisfied – and curious. She could hardly wait for the following Monday, and having put the cottage in order, made her way to the car park behind the row of shops.

She had brushed her hair until it shone, wore her black trousers and a white silk shirt. When she arrived she saw his look of approval, and saw that he was more casually dressed in a polo neck sweater beneath a tweed jacket and matching trousers.

'Ah, Joanna, good morning. Super day to start–'

'Yes – lovely.' The gallery looked different in daylight although there were small lamps and uplighters dotted about, lending a glow to the dark walls. Everywhere smelled of fresh polish, and he saw her look of approval.

'I forgot to mention the rest of the staff,' he smiled. 'A Mrs Tranmore comes in from the village every morning around eight – she has a key, and she dusts and clears up from the day before. She's usually gone by the time we get here. Oh, and there is a lad, a young boy – he's an art student at Reading – he's my odd-job boy. Boles is his name, and he is a boon to have around. He comes in every Saturday, parcels up, lifts things down from the walls, generally will do anything you ask. But I shall be here all this week to give you a hand.'

She noticed that the painting of the garden was still on the easel.

'Come through and sit down,' he said. 'Surprisingly we get quite a few enquiries on Monday, from people who have been browsing during their Sunday walks. Now, if I give you a rough resumé of the stock, and so on, it will help you. Later on, I'll show you the cash till and how to deal with credit cards and so on.'

From a drawer he took a sheaf of papers and laid them on the desk.

'You'll see all the pictures are numbered – the price is on the back and down here. Alongside is the name of the artist and the description of his subject, and then below that is a reference to his – or her – past history; whether the paintings have been hung before. RA means of course that they've been hung in the Royal Academy, or there might be an RWS, meaning the Royal Watercolour Society. There are heaps of reference books here you might like to browse through – that much is up to you – as long as you keep an eye on potential customers – but I thought you might find it interesting.' He looked slightly anxious. 'What do you think?' he asked.

'Well, so far it sounds interesting,' Joanna said.

'Oh, and by the way, if we sell a picture it

gets a small red sticker – they are in here–'

The time was passing quickly, and she sat at the desk provided in the main gallery, feeling free to mooch around and take in as much as she could about this new world she had found herself in.

He suggested she went to lunch at twelve; he himself would go at one, although he often brought a sandwich – it depended on what he had to do.

Halfway through the morning he came out to tell her he had forgotten to show her the kitchen and the cloakroom. She saw that the kitchen had been modernised since the Troubridge days. and not before time, she thought. It had been dark and dreary, and really old-fashioned; now it was modern, with everything to hand. He suggested she make coffee and tea in the afternoon. She went out for a sandwich at twelve and did some shopping and stowed it in the car, and returned quite looking forward to her afternoon. Altogether eleven people came in that day, and one bought a small picture in a wooden frame of an apple.

Hardly exciting, she thought, but I mustn't judge too hastily. It fills a gap, and I don't expect to be here forever.

When she told her mother what she was doing, Linda was surprised. 'You'll be bored stiff, darling,' she said.

'Perhaps – but Gerard is nice,' Joanna said. 'Did you ever meet him?'

'No,' Linda said. 'You were at McAllister Lodge when the agents showed him round and of course the solicitors dealt with the actual sale itself. He paid a good price, you know – although it would have been nice to have kept all the money – but it helped with the liquidation. I'm glad someone nice is living there now.' She couldn't resist a further question. 'Is he married?' she asked. 'Have you–'

'I wouldn't know, Mum,' Joanna replied. 'I just work in the gallery. Well, I must go, 'bye now.'

The time passed uneventfully enough.

During her third week at the gallery, she only saw Gerard once when he came in during the morning, but he had left by lunchtime. She soon learned why Saturday was important, for many people came in to admire – or even to purchase. She had ascertained that the price of the garden scene at McAllister Lodge was sixteen hundred pounds, which at today's prices was not unreasonable but way beyond her pocket. Time was, she reflected, when that would have been nothing; her parents or her husband or her father-in-law would have purchased it without question.

She wondered about Laura, but had not heard anything since she returned from France.

At the end of July, Simon Woodward telephoned and invited her out for dinner. It appeared that Mark Drayton, his New York agent, was coming to England for a few days and would be visiting Simon to discuss his new book, and it was thought that there might be some sort of auction over it. He was quite excited.

'He'll get here on Tuesday, and stay overnight, and I thought if you would join us for a meal at the Drake's Head on Wednesday–'

Joanna was quite excited at the thought of seeing Mark Drayton again.

'He's talked about you – you obviously made an impression,' Simon said, 'so I know he'll be pleased to see you again. I'll pick you up around seven, then we'll have drinks here before going on to the hotel.'

When Gerard called in at the gallery on Thursday afternoon at four, he sensed a quiet excitement about Joanna. Her eyes were bright, and her hair looked as though she had paid a visit to the hairdresser's.

'How is it going?' he said. 'Been busy today?'

'Sold the two small French paintings,' she said, pleased as punch at having made a personal sale.

He was surprised. 'Anyone you know?'

'Well, she looked familiar – I've seen her about often enough.' She didn't tell him that the woman was reputed to be the mother of the late Sir Dennis Davenport's illegitimate son, a fact that had created quite a stir in the neighbourhood. That she knew the woman's mother, Nell Dorgan, since she had worked for the Troubridge family, and that Mandy, for that was her name, had said she had bought a flat locally and needed to furnish it. She liked the little pictures of France and when she knew they had been painted by Laura Troubridge, that settled the matter.

'Oh, good,' Gerard said, wondering what had brought the slight flush to her cheeks and the sparkle to her rather nice eyes.

She glanced up at the clock on the wall.

'Did you wish to leave early?' he asked. 'I'm here, so if you want to go–'

'No, not at all. I've plenty of time. I've been invited out to dinner this evening, so

I'm quite excited – I've lived quietly for so long.'

'Oh,' he murmured, making a mental note that he must do something about that. There was something very attractive about her, not only her looks, but the air of quiet acceptance in everything she did. As if she had been through the mill and come out the other side.

He knew nothing about her private life, only that she was divorced and lived in a cottage not far from what had been her home, the house she had been brought up in, and it gave him a nice feeling.

'Enjoy your evening,' he said. 'You can afford to make it a late night – you don't come in tomorrow.'

'Thank you,' she said.

'Well, I must get back,' he said. 'Good night, Joanna.'

She watched his tall figure as he left – who was he going home to? A wife, a mistress, a partner?

Half an hour later, she locked the door of the gallery and drove home. After putting Ethel away, she went upstairs to bathe and change. She was looking forward to the evening, so seldom did she dine out these days anywhere locally.

She wore a long black silk skirt and a vivid green silk jersey top which brought out the colour of her eyes. Suddenly remembering the long paste emerald earrings her mother had given her, she hurried upstairs to rummage, and found them just as she heard the sound of Simon's car on the drive. Hastily screwing them in with a last look at herself in the mirror, she ran downstairs to open the door.

Simon looked much more rested, as if he had come to terms with the situation, which pleased her. She couldn't have borne to sit with him at dinner in the mood he was in last time she saw him.

He kissed her on both cheeks. 'Joanna – you look wonderful!'

'Thank you,' she said, knowing that she looked her best. Once in the car they drove through the town and up towards Heronsgate. It was a lovely summer evening, and there were plenty of visitors about the town, looking in the shop windows and making for the river, where they would watch the boats queuing at the lock as the water rose and fell while the efficient lockkeeper did his job. It was a never-ending occupation for sightseers.

Driving through the gates of the house,

Joanna could see the river flowing like a wide ribbon, little boats dancing at the jetties. There were great tubs of flowers dotted about the garden – all this being kept up – and for what? Joanna asked herself. Would Laura come back here to live?

Simon led them through to the garden, where, sitting at a table was Mark Drayton, a tray of drinks and bottles in front of him. Her heart leaped at the sight of him; it seemed so odd to see him here, out of context. He jumped up quickly and came forward to greet her, kissing her warmly and standing her at arm's length to look at her.

'You look wonderful!' he said. 'To think there were times when I thought I would never see you again. But fate had something in store for us, I think.'

He smiled at Simon.

'Well – here we are,' Simon said unnecessarily. 'I must do the honours – Mrs Lawrence has gone, as I expect you know,' he said to Joanna. 'Now,' he said, 'I am really on my own.'

Joanna and Mark exchanged a glance.

Joanna took the bull by the horns. 'No word from Laura?' she asked.

He shook his head. 'No.'

He poured champagne for the three of

them and Mark held up his glass. 'To the success of the book,' he said.

He looked into Joanna's eyes and again she felt that *frisson* of pleasure.

There was nothing quite so romantic, she thought, as sitting in this lovely garden drinking champagne with two good-looking men.

'What is the book about?' she asked presently.

'It's a spy thriller,' Simon said. 'My usual – but a little more complicated–'

'You can say that again,' Mark said. 'And we're keeping it under wraps at the moment – it's going to be a huge success, and two or three of the big houses are after it. Hence the auction. The figures being quoted are mind-boggling – and then of course there will be – or should be – the film–'

'Aren't you jumping the gun a bit?' Simon asked. Joanna was pleased. At least all this would take his mind off Laura.

'I don't think so – I know my business,' Mark said. He turned to Joanna. 'And what of you? What are you doing, Joanna? Are you working?'

'I have a new job, although I think it may be only temporary, working for an art gallery.'

He raised his eyebrows.

'Selling art?' he asked. 'I shouldn't have thought that was your thing.'

'It isn't really,' Joanna admitted. 'It's a new gallery – modern art–'

Simon explained. 'This guy took over the old Troubridge shop – antiques – and turned it into a gallery.'

'Is it doing well?'

'Well, I've nothing to compare it with, not knowing the business,' Joanna said. 'But it is quite interesting and I'm learning. It's only a stop-gap until I find something else.'

'Well, here's to the gallery and may it have many sales,' Mark said, looking into her eyes again, and she suddenly remembered the room in the hotel in New York and how close she had come to making love with this man... If the subject of Laura hadn't come up.

The telephone rang inside the house, and Simon got up.

'Excuse me,' he said. 'I've booked the table for eight o'clock – why don't you take Mark for a turn round the garden?' and he went off to answer the phone.

The first flush of the summer roses was over, but the scent from the rose arbour hung on the evening air.

Mark caught her hand, and turned her round to face him. 'Did you think about me when you got home?'

'Yes,' she admitted. 'I did.'

'I certainly thought about you – a lot,' he said. 'More than I've thought about any woman since my wife left me.'

There was so much at stake, Joanna thought swiftly. He was based in America, while her home and her roots were here – how would they ever get together? One of them would have to give up something, but she knew it was not beyond the bounds of possibility. She liked him – felt a rapport with him when he looked at her, but then he was a very good-looking man.

She walked on a bit, still holding his hand.

'Could you ever – I mean – would you ever consider coming to live in the States?' he asked her.

She laughed. 'I hadn't got that far,' she said. 'I liked you and enjoyed being with you so much while I was there–'

He kissed her swiftly on the mouth, and she drew back.

'For starters,' he said.

They heard Simon behind them, and turned to meet him.

His face was ashen.

'It was Laura – she had a son – last night.' He turned away from them. 'They are both well.'

For the second time, Laura had come between them, she and Mark. For the evening was wrecked. With this knowledge, and she presumed Mark had been put in the picture, it could not be the enjoyable evening it had started out to be.

She felt she had to say something. 'I thought the baby was due in August–'

Simon was silent for a time. 'Yes, it was – it was a couple of weeks early, it seems.'

Did that make any difference, Joanna wondered. Laura had been so sure of the timing, but even if it were Simon's, what difference did it make? She was in love with – this Frenchman – always had been. What a mess.

She felt she had to take charge. 'Well – let's go, shall we? Where are you taking me? Somewhere nice, I hope?'

Relieved, Simon looked at her. 'Yes, why not? Sorry, Mark, you seem to have been caught up in – personal problems–'

'No problem,' Mark said succinctly. 'I'm looking forward to my English dinner.'

'Let's take these things back inside,' Joanna said, ever practical. 'Then you can lock up, Simon.'

The things cleared away, Simon locked the outer doors and they drove off in his car towards the Drake's Head.

No-one could have said the evening was a wash-out, for the meal was excellent. But a cloud seemed to hang over the evening – trust Laura, Joanna thought bitterly. Somehow, they talked of this and that – the book, mainly, and its future, and about the gallery, and they were all relieved when it was time to go.

Mark and Joanna walked towards the door while Simon settled the bill.

'Joanna,' Mark said. 'I must see you again.'

'When do you leave?'

'I'm catching the early plane out, tomorrow morning. I have to get back, but I hoped–'

'This is not a good time,' Joanna said. 'Just the luck of the draw, as you might say. Poor old Simon, he's having a rough time.'

'Yeah, I feel sorry for the guy; you win some you lose some. Look,' he said, 'when I get back I'll phone you from New York – and we'll talk about seeing each other again. Will you be coming over to the States again?'

'I'd like to,' she said honestly, thinking

what bad luck it was that the news of Laura's baby should have come now – although she was pleased it was over; now perhaps they could all get on with their lives.

'Ah, there you are,' Simon said. 'How about a nightcap, Joanna?'

'No, I'll get off home if you don't mind dropping me off. I've had a wonderful evening – with two male escorts,' she smiled.

'Sorry I couldn't have been more fun,' Simon said. 'Still, as far as I am concerned, it's another hurdle over.'

He stopped the car outside Saltwater Cottage and Mark got out of the car to see her to the door. He put his arms around her and kissed her, and she was reminded once again of the hotel and how she had nearly–

'I've thought for a long time,' he said, 'that I am falling in love with you. Ever since New York – is there a chance?'

She had to admit his kiss was pleasurable, not breathtaking, but – nice–

'Goodnight Mark,' she said, 'have a good journey,' but her thoughts were of Simon – and Laura...

She slept badly, dozing off and waking from strange dreams, dreams where Laura's baby was confused with the baby expected by Adam's girlfriend, Alise; then she was in a bedroom with Simon, and Gerard was looking at her reproachfully... All the good food and the wine, she supposed, which she was not used to.

It was three-thirty, and she was wide awake. What did she think she was doing with her life? This job, it really wasn't for her. She was bored with it, truth to tell, and only stayed on because she liked Gerard. The business as such had no appeal for her; the days were long, she wanted some kind of life, and it wasn't this one...

She finally got to sleep about four in the morning and was awakened by the doorbell ringing at eight-thirty.

Slipping on a dressing gown, she hurried downstairs, and unlocked the door to find Simon standing there. He looked awful.

'May I come in?' he asked.

'Of course,' Joanna said, leading the way into the small kitchen, then putting the kettle on.

'I remember you said you didn't have to go into work today, and I don't think I've slept a wink,' he said. 'I've tossed and turned all night. I still can't believe it – suppose it's really my baby, Joanna, what then?'

He turned to her and put his arms around her, hugging her tightly. 'Oh, Joanna – what a mess!'

He lowered his eyes to hers. He just needed bodily comfort, she told herself. The need to hold on to someone, for consolation – she knew the feeling well. Time was when she would have given anything for this, his two arms around her.

She eased him gently away. 'Sit down – I'll make the coffee.'

His head was bowed in his hands.

She couldn't possibly know, she thought, about the timing of the baby. It was none of her business – did he think it was possible it could be his? And what if it was? It made no difference in the long run.

She placed a steaming cup of coffee in front of him. 'Drink this,' she said, her heart going out to him.

'You are such a dear friend,' he said. 'I don't know what I would have done without you.

Now, she thought, not without a gleam of humour, I could have two men in my life.

Three days later, Laura telephoned her from France. She sounded so excited, like her old self. 'Jo? Jo? It's me, Laura, did Simon tell you? I have a baby son, oh, Joanna

217

– he is so beautiful – seven pounds – are you there? Joanna?'

'Yes, congratulations. I'm so pleased for you.'

There was a short silence, then Laura said: 'I know I've behaved badly – to you – and Simon, and to tell you the truth, Jo – I wouldn't admit it to anyone else – I think it's Simon's baby–' and she heard the gasp from the other end. 'Don't hate me too much, I could be wrong, but he is like Simon – and you know what, Jo? It doesn't make any difference, I'd never go back to him. My life is here. Jo? Joanna? Can you hear me?'

'Yes, I hear you,' Joanna said coldly. 'But I have to go, Laura. Congratulations – stay well – 'bye.'

She put down the telephone, and much to her surprise, burst into tears.

Chapter Fourteen

Louise Rivers and Mandy Davis met up in Buckham High Street at the supermarket. They were at the fruit counter, and glanced at each other as they both chose apples. One paled and the other's cheeks went a fiery red.

Mandy stood in shock, open-mouthed; it was the first time she had met a member of the Davenport family since the funeral and the reading of the Will, and for Louise, the first time she had met Mandy as the mother of her half-brother.

Louise spoke first.

'Mandy–' she spoke softly and Mandy bit her lip. She had never felt so embarrassed in her life, but she was grateful that it was Louise and not either of the other two. Not likely, she thought, Lady Davenport shopping for apples.

'Louise,' she said, her colour coming back. 'How are you?'

'I'm fine,' Louise said. 'And you?'

'Fine,' Mandy answered, glad she had got her dark suit on and had had her hair cut and restyled. These days you might not have known her, so different was her lifestyle, her thinking.

Louise approved of what she saw. This was a different Mandy, quite unlike the image of the cleaning lady she carried in her mind. A swift observation of the cut of Mandy's suit, the make-up and the hairdo, the expensive handbag. A little bitterly, she recalled the generous settlement, but she was by nature a kind young woman, and although twenty years Mandy's junior, still had a healthy respect for her.

'Look,' she said. 'Fancy a coffee?'

Mandy took the bull by the horns. 'Yes – that would be nice. Where shall we go?'

'Pity they don't have one in here. What about the corner coffee shop, the Green Door? Half an hour, fifteen minutes?'

Mandy was anxious to get the meeting over with. 'Say twenty minutes – see you there, then.'

She did no more shopping, but joined the queue to pay her bill, seeing Louise at the other check-out, and decided that the sooner she got this over, the better. It was bound to happen sometime.

She ordered coffee and sat waiting and soon Louise appeared. She had put her shopping in the car while Mandy, who had not much, for her mother did most of the shopping, put the plastic bag on a chair together with her handbag.

They both sat with coffee in front of them, then smiled across at each other – a weak smile, but nevertheless one that denoted if not friendship, then understanding.

Louise took a deep breath. 'Well, I

suppose this was bound to happen sooner or later,' she said. 'I wonder we haven't bumped into each other before.'

'I don't come to the shops very often,' Mandy said. Even her voice was slightly different, more ladylike, Louise thought, or was that imagination?

'Well, tell me how you are,' she said, still, Mandy thought, in charge of the situation.

'I'm very well,' Mandy said, 'and how are you?' The conversation was stilted, as Louise knew it would be, and she decided to break the ice; it was ridiculous, skating around the edge of things. She had always believed in coming to the point.

'How is Tom getting on?' Her eyes were wide and friendly.

'Oh, he's fine. He was twelve last month.'

'Goodness,' Louise murmured, and wondered whether Nell Dorgan had ever told Mandy she had called.

Mandy clicked open her handbag, and brought out a small envelope.

Yes, there he was, his features indelibly printed on Louise's mind.

'He's a handsome lad,' she said. 'A credit to you, Mandy.'

Mandy's face flamed. 'Thank you. He's like his father, isn't he?'

'Yes, he is – like he was at that age.'

Mandy began to relax, deciding that there was nothing anyone could do about it now. She had always liked Louise – no reason not to be friendly.

'Are you – staying with your mother?' Mandy asked. 'At Davenport House?'

What memories she's got of that, Louise thought bitterly. 'Yes, I'm staying there – have been for some time.'

Mandy for the life of her couldn't ask about Lady Davenport, so instead she asked about Helen.

'Oh, she's fine – pregnant – they've moved up to Shropshire.'

'That's nice,' Mandy said. Although she didn't know it at all.

'So – what are you doing now, Mandy?' Louise asked at length. She began to wish she hadn't suggested this but it had to be done sometime or other.

'Well, firstly, I've moved house.'

This did surprise Louise. 'Oh, really – where?'

'To a place called Dudley Court – it's just outside Buckham on the road to–'

'I know it,' Louise said. 'Goodness, that's rather nice, isn't it?'

'It's been turned into apartments,' Mandy

said, 'and I bought one of them – a down-stairs apartment; the grounds are lovely, and it's quite near the river. It will be nice for Tom to go outside in the grounds and I don't have the worry of a garden to see to.'

That must have cost an arm and a leg, thought Louise, but then what the hell, this woman was comparatively rich.

'I had to think of Tom,' Mandy said seriously. 'We've been living with Mum all this time, but I had to get out sooner or later for his sake.'

The tension between them suddenly evaporated.

'Oh, I'm so glad, Mandy. You know, you look wonderful,' and it was clear she meant it.

She thought how pretty Mandy was, at fiftyish – no wonder her father had found her attractive – but, she thought a little vindictively, she suspected he had thought that about a great many women. She had had no suspicions before, except those one would normally have about a very good-looking man with plenty of charm; but after the funeral, and all those women there – you couldn't tell her they were all past members of staff. Still, it was water under the bridge now – they all had to face facts.

'I loved your father,' Mandy said suddenly, and for a usually tough girl, Louise felt like weeping.

'I am sure you did,' she said.

'I suppose I thought he was the greatest thing since sliced bread,' Mandy smiled ruefully. 'When my husband died, I was still quite young, somehow couldn't imagine getting married again – and your father was very kind–'

I bet, thought Louise.

'I – we – I never thought it would all come out. We kept it a secret for so long–'

'You certainly did,' Louise agreed. 'So Tom has been living with your parents and you all this time?'

'Yes. I moved last week, and it really is lovely. Of course, Tom is at school at Stansford Gate, but next autumn he will be going to Eton. He has passed his entrance exam,' she added proudly. 'I took him – oh, it is such a wonderful school – of course that was your father's idea – he put him down when he was born.'

He would, Louise thought, a chip off the old block.

'So life has changed for you, Mandy.'

'Very much so,' Mandy said.

'Have you told him – anything about – er–'

'On his birthday, I explained to him, as best as I could. After all, his name is not the same as mine, so I had some explaining to do.'

'What did he say?'

'Nothing – at that age, I don't think it means that much. Or if it does, he keeps it to himself. I told him what a great man his father was.'

'Did he ask about the Davenport family, I mean, if there were any others?'

'No, nothing. I'll always answer questions truthfully when he does, but I think it should come from him first.'

'Very sensible,' Louise said.

Mandy was dying to know what Louise was doing here and how Lady Davenport was, but couldn't bring herself to ask.

'I'd love to see him,' Louise said swiftly. 'After all, he is my half-brother–'

'Yes, I realise that,' Mandy said. 'Well, I don't see why not,' and she saw her opening. 'Would your mother mind that?'

'She's not around,' Louise said shortly.

Mandy frowned. 'Not around – what do you mean?'

Louise took a deep breath. 'After the funeral she announced her intention of going away – abroad – she hardly talked to us – you must imagine what it has been like for her.'

'I do,' Mandy said. 'I never thought it would ever come out.'

'You couldn't keep a thing like that secret for ever,' Louise said reprovingly. 'It was bound to come out sooner or later. It was such a shock to my mother, such a disaster in more ways than one, that she almost went into a decline. We saw little of her, she shut herself away, and then told us, she had no interest in Davenport House, that it would be going to Tom at some point, but that we could live in it if we wanted to, but she had no interest in it. A week later, she had packed and gone.'

Mandy was horrified. 'Louise! Where is she?'

'We had a card from Paris – then nothing – it's as if she has cut herself off from everyone in England.'

Mandy saw that her eyes had filled with tears. So unlike Louise, who was the tough one.

She put a hand on her arm. 'Oh, Louise, I'm sorry. I had no idea.'

'Of course you hadn't,' Louise said, blowing her nose and pulling herself together. 'How could you? But when things – like this – are done, many people get hurt.'

'In other words, you open a can of worms.'

'Well, I wouldn't put it as harshly as that – still.'

Well, Mandy thought, defending herself. It takes two – and Lady Davenport – but she wouldn't think about that now. It was all in the past.

'I suppose everyone reacts in the way that is natural to them. Helen is on my mother's side. She always was. I keep most things to myself, but I can understand Mummy's point of view. She was just unable to take it, and dealt with it in her own way.'

They sat for a moment. Then Mandy got to her feet and picked up her handbag and carrier bag. 'I think I'd better go,' she said. 'It really was nice seeing you. I live at No. 2 Dudley Court – anytime you feel like getting in touch–'

'Thank you,' Louise said.

Mandy could not bring herself to say, regards to your mother or Helen – how could she?

Head high, she walked towards the cash desk and paid for the coffee, then turned and, with a little wave, left the shop.

Lady Davenport, Julia, had had a brother. A handsome boy, and an even more handsome young man. He was clever, too, brilliant, and he went to Oxford and had a great career in front of him. Everyone expected it.

Julia's mother had always wanted a son, and he was blatantly her favourite. She was fond of her daughter, but beside the incredible Charles, Julia must automatically take a back seat.

When he was twenty-one, up at Oxford, he met a young barmaid. She was as pretty as a picture, nineteen, well known to all the young men in the town and what Julia's mother, had she used such a word, would have called 'tarty'.

Charles fell in love with her, hopelessly, and dared to take her home.

Julia's mother, Mrs Casemore, took one look at the girl and almost fainted.

But young Charles was adamant. He had the looks, he had the brains, and the stubbornness that goes with knowing that, and at the end of a month, he left his home, left Oxford behind him, and went by ship to Australia, taking Melanie Summers with him.

They never saw nor heard from him again. His name was never to be mentioned. From that day, Mrs Casemore changed. Her very nice blue eyes were cold, like chips of ice, without expression. When some years later she became a widow, after Julia had married, she lived the life of a recluse.

Pity for what had been racked Julia, and once she asked her mother: 'Don't you wonder sometimes about Charles, Mummy? Wonder how he is? Perhaps he has a family, you might have grandchildren.'

Mrs Casemore turned her lined and empty face towards the window. 'You can forget anything, if you've a mind to. Blot it out of your thoughts – bury it – and it's dead.'

After that, Julia never mentioned her brother again.

But now, her mother's words came back to her. Blot it out – believe it never happened; her mother had proved it; that day – the funeral – she had imagined it.

So strong was her willpower, she never allowed herself to think about it – she must plan for the future, her future. She had no qualms; the children were old enough to live their own lives, but she – she had a life in front of her. And she must use her brains. She did not intend to waste her life as her mother had.

She took very little with her, personal jewellery and a few possessions, including her exquisite mink coat which she got out of storage, knowing that women in France and Italy and Europe did not feel quite the same as did the women of England about women wearing furs, the skins of animals.

When she arrived in Paris, she booked into the Ritz Hotel and shopped until she dropped and bought Louis Vuitton luggage wherein to put it all. From an agency she engaged a personal lady's maid – for they were still to be found in France – a woman who was impressed with her title and who recognised in that beautiful face a determination to be reckoned with.

She could do worse than throw in her lot with this English lady.

Then Lady Davenport and Nicole Deschamps flew to Rome.

She booked into the finest and most expensive hotel in the city; after all, if you aimed high, it must be to secure the richest catch. A chauffeur carried her expensive luggage in, and her lady's maid carried her furs. At the reception desk, an army of uniformed men almost bowed before this vision – although they were used to the most famous clientele in the world. Elderly gentlemen sitting in the luxurious deep armchairs raised their eyebrows above their newspapers and made a mental note: of the woman herself, who was beautiful, of her retinue; and they noted everything about her, her carriage, her beauty, and the fact that she was not a modern young thing tasting the sights and sounds of Rome for the first time. No rich young pop star, not of the avant-garde, but a woman who knew her way about, a woman who knew what she wanted. A rich widow, they decided. No divorcee – who would want to leave a woman like that?

Within half an hour, everyone who was anyone knew who she was. Lady Julia Davenport, recently widowed, from London, England.

The maid, Nicole, Julia discovered, was a treasure. She knew about hair, which was the most important thing, for Julia had abundant hair which needed to be dressed. She knew about eye make-up too, but there was nothing she could teach Julia about that. She had been using her violet eyes ever since she had discovered them at the age of ten, when an elderly uncle had told her mother that 'Julia has the most beautiful eyes I have ever seen'.

When she walked into the dining room that evening all eyes were upon her. She was escorted to her own table for one, the best seat in the room by a potted palm, dressed in a long pale pink dress (one of Balenciaga's) which fitted her like a glove, for she had lost weight. She wore her pearls and drop pearl earrings, a foil for the cloud of silvery hair which looked almost platinum blonde, which made a perfect frame for her face. She looked around forty-five instead of the fifty-five she was, and she knew it.

She ate sparely and delicately, seeing no one, and after refusing coffee in the adjoining lounge, she made her way to the lift and up to the first floor, where Nicole sat waiting for her.

She slipped off her silver sandals, while Nicole turned back the sheets and plumped the pillows.

'I shall go to bed early, Nicole,' she said. 'You may take the rest of the evening off. I shall breakfast in my room – did you tell them that?'

'Oui, madame,' Nicole said.

'Now tell me who is staying here,' Julia said.

Nicole had been busy. She was able in a very short time to tell Julia who was who and from where. Potted histories followed. She had been working in the capital cities of

Europe for twenty years and knew her subject.

The days passed, one much like another. A visit to the hairdresser, to the beauty salon, to the wonderful shops of Rome, perhaps a stroll in the gardens, a rest – and dressing for dinner. Men of different ages and nationalities introduced themselves to her; she sometimes took pre-dinner drinks with them, always dressed in some incomparable gown, but the general impression she gave was one of distant unavailability.

Having tired of Rome, it was in this mood that she and Nicole set off for Venice, where they booked into the Cipriano. From her balcony she looked down at the waters of the canal, the gondoliers and vaporetti, the low voices reaching up to her in her luxurious apartment. She felt more at home here – and settled herself in. There were all sorts of nationalities: French, Italian, American, Australians – many with their overfed wives, or younger versions, stick-thin, ever watchful, with calculating eyes on their menfolk while pretending not to be. Julia observed it all with cold violet eyes – she saw it all.

She could not fault the Cipriano, the food was excellent, the service perfect, but there were far too many accompanied men. Julia was not a husband-stealer, she knew exactly the sort of man she was looking for; he need not be excessively wealthy, although it would help, for she had enough money of her own. The only thing she knew for sure was that she never wished to return to England to live.

So with this in mind she moved on; she would go to the south of France. There were many in Julia's position there, but she could stand competition. So sure of herself was she.

With Nicole and her luggage she arrived in Nice, knowing she could move along the coast if she had a mind. At least the weather was kinder, and the sun shone down on the Promenade des Anglais, and her violet eyes held just the faintest glimmer of interest.

Back home in Buckham, Mandy unlocked the front door of her parents' home.

'Only me!' she called, and Nell's pleasant smile grew wider.

'Just called in for a minute,' Mandy said. 'Where's Dad?'

'Gone down to the Swan,' Nell said. 'He said for a game of billiards.'

'Oh, yes,' Mandy said. 'Well, you will never guess–'

'Then don't keep me in suspense,' Nell said.

'I bumped into – Louise – Louise Davenport – Louise Rivers.'

Nell went white.

'You didn't!'

'I did,' Mandy repeated.

'Whatever did you do?'

Mandy flopped down in an easy chair. 'Well,' she was enjoying this while Nell worried that Louise had told about her earlier visit.

'We ended up talking, and having a coffee, in the Green Door.'

'You never!'

'We did,' and she proceeded to tell her mother all of it exactly as it happened.

'Well!' Nell said. 'Who'd have thought it?'

'Can't think why it never happened before.'

'Did she mention – her mother?' She hardly liked to mention Lady Davenport by name.

'What about this then? Her mother's gone.'

'Gone? Gone where?'

'Louise says they don't know. Says her mother took it very badly, and announced her intention of leaving them, and said she wouldn't be coming back.'

'What rubbish,' Nell said. 'That's just like her, frightening those girls to death – all that acting–'

'Louise seemed to think she meant it. A few days later she'd gone, taking hardly anything with her, and said she would be going to Italy first, but then they had a card from Paris and nothing since.'

'Oh, she's a wicked woman,' Nell said. 'Those poor girls – to walk out on them–'

'Takes all sorts, Mum.'

'You're right there, my girl,' Nell said, pursing her lips.

Chapter Fifteen

The tears she had shed that night, Joanna realised later, were for a lost friendship. Nothing would ever be the same again – it was like a broken love affair. True friendship should survive anything, but she realised now that she could never have really known Laura. Their values were obviously different. She was no angel herself, had made mistakes, but she could never have done what

Laura had done to Simon.

She turned up for work at the gallery next morning, feeling drained. After Laura's call the previous evening, she had lain awake, wondering what the outcome of it all would be, and discovering that she really didn't care anymore. Laura was the sort of person who would do what she wanted to do, when she wanted to – no matter how many people got hurt. She also realised that if it were not for nice Gerard, she wouldn't stay in this job. It had been a stop-gap, but nothing else. She was no more geared to selling paintings than Laura had been to antiques, more's the pity. For Gerard was nice, attractive, they got on well and she admired him. But she needed more to fill her days. Even the work at the surgery had been more interesting, and there was a satisfaction about it.

She decided that so much had taken place in the past year that she was beyond thinking straight. Far better hold on for a while until she got herself sorted out. Her thoughts often went out to her trip to America and how wonderful that had been. Seeing her aunt had been wonderful, but meeting Mark Drayton had been even nicer.

She missed a man in her life, and wondered if she would ever again feel what she had for Adam. If he hadn't met that girl, they might have been married by now, and had–

But that was wishful thinking. Her mother had been right: he was too young for her. It was an interlude. Put it in perspective.

There were few browsers this morning, and when the telephone rang at eleven, she was grateful for a distraction. She swallowed hard when she heard Simon's voice.

'Joanna? Do you mind my ringing you during business hours? I'll call later if you like–'

'No, I'm not busy. How are you?'

'So-so, Joanna. I wondered if you would do something for me?' Her heart sank. Would this business never end?

'If I can.'

'Will you have dinner with me this evening? We'll go out – or have something in.'

She thought swiftly. 'Come to me. I'll get something on my way home.'

'Are you sure?'

'Yes, quite sure. Do you fancy anything in particular?'

'No, anything you like. I'll bring the wine.'

'No need,' Joanna smiled. 'Say around seven – time for a drink beforehand.'

She put down the phone. She was glad to

have something to do – although she would be pleased when this on-going saga was over.

She had a quick lunch and shopped for the evening. Gerard did not put in an appearance today, so she locked the doors behind her and drove home to Saltwater Cottage.

She laid the table and opened the red wine – there was a bottle of white in the fridge – and saw to the vegetables and dessert.

She heard the car on the drive and went to open the door, pleased to see that Simon looked more rested, as though he had come to terms with the situation. He had brought a bottle of wine, and he kissed her and put his arm through hers.

'You're a brick,' he said. 'I'd like you to know that – all through this miserable business–'

'Well, you are the one going through it all,' Joanna said.

She led him through to the small living room, where she had set out glasses on a tray.

'What would you like, red or white, gin and tonic?'

'Red wine, thanks,' he said, sitting himself down in what had once been Adam's chair.

When they were both settled, Joanna smiled at him. 'Now – to what do I owe this unexpected pleasure?' she asked.

'Well–' He spoke slowly. 'I wanted to see you before I left.'

'You're leaving?'

'Yes – at the weekend, and I wanted to tell you first.'

'Is this a sudden decision?'

'Yes – made after a phone call from Laura last evening. She is coming in three weeks' time, bringing the baby – don't ask me why, but she obviously has a lot to see to. I don't want to see her, to be around when she comes. So I'm moving out – and I shall sue for divorce, which my solicitors will advise her on, if they haven't already done so.'

'Golly,' Joanna said. 'Does she know you will have gone?'

'I have no intention of telling her. Isn't that the way it is done in her family – you do what you want to do and ask questions afterwards?'

There was no answer to that. Of course he was feeling bitter, and why not, Joanna thought – an eye for an eye...

'I shall go back to the flat; after all, nothing here belongs to me except my personal possessions.'

Joanna frowned.

'Why do you look like that?'

'I don't know, it's sad, that's all, that it should have come to this.'

'And whose fault is that?' he asked reasonably.

He has accepted it, Joanna thought. 'Just let me check the oven,' she said, excusing herself.

In the kitchen she stood for a moment. What an end to it all, she thought – but what was the alternative?

Back in the living room, she sat down again. 'Anything you'd like me to do?'

'That's sweet of you, Joanna.'

He looked at her over his glass. 'You know when I first met you, I thought you were the one–' and Joanna found herself flushing to the tips of her ears.

'Oh.'

'I did. I thought we had something going there for a while, but then Laura arrived – and well, I just fell for her – hook, line and sinker, you might say.'

You might indeed, Joanna thought.

'Still – that's all water under the bridge now, but no reason why we can't be friends. I am still very fond of you, Joanna.'

And suddenly Joanna didn't want to hear

any more.

'Excuse me, I think that's the timer–'

She simmered down in the kitchen and returned with another smile.

'Almost ready,' she said.

'Well, there's no reason why we can't meet up now and again, is there?' he asked, his lovely dark eyes looking straight into hers.

I hope, Joanna mused, you cannot read my thoughts. 'Of course not,' she said, almost heartily.

'I like to think all this hasn't made any difference to our friendship. You've been wonderful, and I am so grateful.'

What have we here, Joanna wondered. The makings of a slightly pompous elderly man. 'That's what friends are for,' she said inanely – and was suddenly very grateful that he hadn't chosen her.

She had it in her heart to almost feel sorry for Laura; apart from his writing and his books, which were so successful, Simon probably had no time for anything else. She must have felt life was very constricting with him – boring even; still, that didn't excuse what she had done.

He put his arms round her and kissed her when he left, and she wasn't sorry to see him go.

Closing the door after him, she took a deep breath. She need never see him again, she thought. As for Laura, she would be away when she arrived from France – at Leamington Spa, she thought. Laura would be bound to advise her when she was coming – yes, that's what she would do.

A week later she had a call from New York, and she knew who it would be, her heart beating wildly as she recognised Mark's voice.

'Joanna – any chance of seeing you?' he asked.

She thought he was referring to another trip to the States. 'Oh, Mark, I don't–'

'I'm coming over,' he said. 'Can I see you?'

'Of course you can – when?' she asked.

'You are not going to believe this, but we're opening a branch in London, and I've put in for the job – how do you feel about that?'

Oh, goodness! she thought. Nothing would please her more.

'I've got to look over these premises, some-where in Canary Wharf, I think; anyway, I shall be over for a few days, three at least, probably next week sometime when I get through here.'

She tried to still her heart, which was

fluttering with excitement. She hadn't realised just how much he meant to her.

'I'll give you a call when I'm leaving – OK?'

'Yes, that's fine,' she said, and when she put the phone down her green eyes positively shone.

There was yet another surprise in store for her on her next working day when Gerard called in and asked her to Sunday lunch. 'I wondered how you would feel about seeing your old home with someone else living in it?'

'Curious, I think,' she laughed. She was in a good mood these days, he thought. Had perked up quite a bit.

'Come about twelve-thirty,' he said. 'We usually eat at one – there is someone I'd like you to meet.'

She opened wide eyes to his.

'See you then,' he said. 'Have to rush now.'

Well, Joanna thought, she would look forward to that. Her social life was looking up. For a couple of days now she had not even thought about Laura.

On a lovely September morning Joanna unlocked the garage doors, and drove Ethel out for the ten-minute drive to McAllister Lodge. How strange it felt, driving along such familiar lanes; she could see the tall chimneys of the house, while the trees and the hedgerows were still in high summer. There were few birds now but she saw a small rabbit stop for a moment, quite still, as it heard the sound of a car, then scuttle away through the undergrowth. The trees were lovely, and as she approached the house it was if she had never left it.

The door was opened in answer to her ring by Gerard, and it seemed so strange to see him out of context, particularly in her old house. He took her hand and kissed her lightly on the cheek and she could see already that it was a very different setting. For one thing, the soft fawn carpet had gone and now there were polished wooden floors and rugs, and the walls were dark – and although it was interesting, it was not the same house. There were paintings every-where, so that it all resembled the gallery rather than McAllister Lodge. Through to the large drawing room – her mother's pride and joy, the room that overlooked the river, which even now shone – she could see a couple of swans elegantly gliding on the glit-tering water. There were blinds now, drawn against the sun, she imagined to keep the brightness off the pictures, and the furniture was as modern as anything she would ever see.

She smiled, though, because it was attractive, though different, and she could see he was anxious for her approval.

'Oh, Gerard, it's lovely! Different – but most attractive,' and she saw the relief on his face.

'I think it's always difficult to see your old home with someone else's possessions – anyway, I'm glad you approve. Would you care for a drink? Martini?

'That would be nice.'

It was so long since she had had a Martini; not since her father was alive, she was sure. He mixed it now, giving it to her in the flat, cone-like glass.

'Please sit down,' he said, and she sat on one of the enormous sofas and noticed that the marble fireplace was the same. She wasn't sure if she was pleased or not that she had come.

He joined her on the other end of the sofa and presently there was a tap on the door and it was pushed open, and in came the girl Joanna had seen before; a pretty girl, but now she was holding the hand of a small girl, who was so like Gerard it was obvious that she was his daughter.

'Thank you, Lilli,' he said, and Lilli let go of the little girl's hand.

The little girl, who was about five, smiled and jumped on to her father's lap. 'Daddy!' she said.

He kissed her. 'This is Sophie, my daughter. And this, Sophie, is Joanna – Joanna McAllister.'

'Hallo, Sophie.'

Sophie's eyes widened. 'Like McAllister Lodge.'

'Yes – Joanna's father built this house, and Joanna grew up here.'

'I am going to grow up here,' Sophie said, and climbed down from her father's knee and went back to Lilli. She looked rather shy.

'Lilli, take Sophie back now, and see how Mrs Warren is getting on. I think we will be eating at one. See you later, darling.'

When the door had closed behind them, he turned to Joanna.

'I have Sophie at weekends – that's why I'm always busy on a Saturday. Cigarette?'

Joanna shook her head.

He lit one, and blew out the match.

'My wife and I are divorced; she lives in London, and has remarried. Lilli lives with them – she's Norwegian, and looks after

Sophie – altogether, it's quite a sensible arrangement, works quite well. I'm fortunate that I do at least get Sophie for weekends.'

Joanna could not have been more surprised at the set-up; it was nothing like she had imagined. She had never thought of him as a family man.

'I used to live in London, as I think I told you, but I wanted to get out into the country more, and I knew this house would be wonderful for Sophie at weekends, and in the summer holidays.'

The dining room was even more modern, with its dark green walls and ultra modern furniture; so unlike her parents' dining room, it was difficult to imagine it was the same room.

'What do you think of it all?' Gerard asked her during lunch.

'Well,' she said slowly. 'It is so different that I can't imagine it's the same house. It's amazing what you can do with a change of décor.'

He looked pleased. 'Yes. We must go round the garden after lunch. Lilli goes off for the afternoon, then later, around six, she will drive Sophie back to London.'

Quite a ménage, Joanna decided. She had

not been unaware of Lilli's looks of adoration at Gerard. Joanna guessed that she was around twenty-five, and wondered if anything was going on between them. The situation was so different from what she had imagined in the gallery; even McAllister Lodge was nothing like her old home.

They walked round the garden, taking Sophie with them. She ran on ahead, and played among the paths and terraces. Poor little girl, Joanna thought – she had always thought broken marriages where children were concerned were sad. The garden at least was familiar, seeing the scene that Gerard had painted, and she felt her throat constrict.

They had tea during Lilli's absence, and Joanna read to Sophie, who, now the ice was broken, was quite a chatterbox. Gerard seemed delighted that they got on so well, but Joanna felt guilty. Guilty at the thoughts she had sometimes had during sleepless nights, when she had imagined being back at McAllister Lodge again, perhaps with Gerard – that was until she had seen the girl, Lilli, and then she had wondered about his private life.

Now, she knew, whatever Gerard's problem was, it had nothing to do with her. McAllister Lodge had gone, for ever, and

Gerard – well, Gerard was a very nice man who had problems – and there was nothing there that she could solve.

Before she left, Gerard took her to his studio, the two large rooms which had constituted the loft, usually filled with storage and unwanted furniture. Now it had been cleaned out, for it had a north light, and painted, and was stacked with paintings and easels and the accoutrements of an artist – it was as if McAllister Lodge had been given a new lease of life.

'I must go,' she said presently. 'I have enjoyed it, Gerard. You have done it all beautifully – very artistic – and I hope you will be very happy here.'

Sophie had obviously taken a fancy to her, and kissed her shyly. 'Will you come again?' she asked.

'If I'm asked,' Joanna smiled.

Who knew what the future held?

When the phone call came from New York the following week, it was Mark to say he was catching the overnight plane and would arrive at Heathrow the next day.

'I'll be there to meet you,' Joanna said.

'Oh, Joanna, there's no need; I'll take a taxi.'

'I'll check with arrivals, so don't worry, I'll be there.'

'I can't wait to see you.'

'Me too,' Joanna said, and meant it.

When Mark arrived out of customs the following week, it was to a Joanna whose eyes shone green with a brilliance he hadn't seen before. She was holding out a placard which read MARK!

He grinned and hugged her to him, and they kissed for a long time, oblivious to the passers-by – and Joanna knew she had never been happier. Taking his hand, she led him towards the car park, where Ethel sat waiting.

'What's this?' he said, looking down at her.

'This is Ethel,' she said. 'My good companion.'

He managed to tuck his long legs into the passenger seat.

'Where are we going?' he asked, as she started off towards the check-out.

She turned laughing eyes to his. 'Saltwater Cottage,' she said. 'Where else?'

'I've never seen the inside of your house,' Mark said.

She smiled. 'Well, there's a first time for everything.'

And if you interrupt me this time, Laura, she promised, I'll kill you.

Chapter Sixteen

Mandy sat on a seat by the river, watching the swans and the eider ducks, the mandarins with their wonderful colours, looking for all the world as though they came straight out of a Chinese opera. This was such a peaceful spot and she was so pleased she had decided to move here.

The apartment was spacious and roomy after her parents' house, and although she hadn't finished furnishing it yet, she knew it would be even better when she had.

Strange how she had ended up here – somewhere she couldn't have envisaged in her wildest dreams. And all because of Tom, the light of her life. She would go through it all over again if it meant that she could give birth to Tom. Not, she thought, that it hadn't been fraught with worry at the time. She hadn't given a damn about Lady Davenport's feelings – and neither apparently had Dennis – the worst thing had been having to tell Nell she was pregnant.

Their rendezvous had been in a little hotel

further up river, a pretty place, hidden, or so they hoped, away from the madding crowds, whenever Dennis could manage it. He always had the excuse for being away overnight on business, and she was only too pleased to meet him.

What a lover! Nothing in her married life had given her so much pleasure – although she had loved her husband and was sad when he died so young. But Dennis was something else. He knew how to pleasure a woman – she had found that expression somewhere in a book, and thought that described it perfectly.

When Tom was born, Dennis was thrilled. 'A son!' he had said over and over again. 'Mandy,' he said. 'I'll give you the moon!'

She smiled now. Well, he had, in a way. Paid for everything; she had had the baby in an exclusive nursing home in London, he had paid her a good allowance – there was nothing Tom wanted for, private schools all paid for. Oh, Dennis was so proud of him.

Even now, she could feel no pity for her ladyship. She disliked her intensely; she had only kept on working at Davenport House because she liked the girls and the house and of course – Dennis.

On reflection, she tried to feel what it

must be like to learn as Lady Davenport had the details of her husband's private life, but she couldn't raise any sympathy for her. She was a spoiled woman, who exploited Dennis, and she was glad that she had been able to provide a little light relief, as it were.

A man passed by on the towpath with a small dog on a lead, and nodded to her. This was private, the grounds of Dudley Court, he must be a resident. She might get a dog, Tom would like that, and it would be company for her. A boat came by, idling, two women lying in bikinis on deck, the man at the wheel. She could have mooring here, but had no interest in boats. Tom may have, later. It was pleasant, sitting here daydreaming; she had never been nor felt so idle in her life. It didn't suit her, because she was by nature an active woman. But she had made up her mind to do things, learn things, if only for Tom.

She had joined the Buckham Country Club; very exclusive, fees costing an arm and a leg, but she would be able to take Tom there to lunch on a Sunday. They also had a keep-fit class which she had joined, although she hadn't been yet. She was taking elocution lessons, and she might, just might, take French lessons; after all, when Tom was at Eton she would have plenty of time to herself and who knows, they might take a trip to France in the holidays. Dennis would be pleased if she did that.

'Excuse me – may I?' and she turned to find a man smiling down at her.'

Shaken out of her reverie. She smiled back at him. 'Of course.'

'Thank you,' and he sat down. He was nice-looking, around sixty, and she recognised him as the man who had pipped her to the post at number 1.

'Edwin Carpenter,' he said, holding out his hand. 'It's time we met, isn't it?'

She took his hand. It was a firm handshake; she liked that.

'Miranda Dorgan,' she said, 'although most people call me Mandy.'

'I like Miranda,' he said. 'It's an unusual name. You live in number 2, don't you?'

He had rather nice hazel eyes, behind tortoiseshell glasses, regular features, and a friendly smile. All this she took in in the space of a second or two, before looking back to the river.

'Yes, I was lucky to get it. I would have liked the one you have, but you pipped me to the post,' and she smiled to show no ill feeling.

They stopped talking to watch an eight going past, the rowers in unison, such beauty of movement as the oars skimmed the water, every man giving every ounce of his strength.

Edwin sighed. 'Wonderful,' he said, then turned to her again.

'You live alone?' he asked.

'I have a son, he's going on thirteen. He's at day school at the moment – next year, of course, he will board.'

'Wonderful time,' he said and looked back at the river. 'My wife died two years ago, and I have a family, two girls and a boy; they are all married, but come to stay with me occasionally.'

Which is why he wanted the larger flat, Mandy decided.

'That's nice for you,' Mandy said.

'Yes, I love their visits – don't see much of them. One is in Africa, one in Scotland and the other lives in London. I have five grandchildren, so far–' and he smiled.

The man walking the dog returned from his walk and nodded over to them. Quite a friendly place, Mandy decided.

'You are a widow?' Edwin asked.

'Yes,' Mandy said. 'I've been a widow for many years.'

'It's hard living alone, isn't it?'

'I lived with my parents for quite some time, but now Tom is older I need somewhere of my own.'

'I think we made a good choice, coming here,' Edwin said. 'It's a beautiful spot, and they converted the house very well. It used to belong to a shipping magnate who built it in 1898.'

'I love it,' Mandy said. 'I always wanted to live by the river.'

'I – we – lived at Bray,' Edwin said.

'Oh, that's a lovely spot.'

'Yes, we bought it when we first married. But it was too big – with the children gone and my wife–'

'You were there a long time, then,' Mandy said. 'It must have been a wrench to leave it.'

'Yes, it was. But you have to move on. Life changes. Then you adapt.'

That's true, Mandy thought. That's what life is about. Accepting and adapting.

'You must come in and see my flat – although, of course, you have already seen it.'

'Not furnished,' Mandy said. 'And it makes such a difference, doesn't it? I haven't finished mine yet, but there's no hurry, I'm taking my time.'

'Good for you,' he said. 'Er – how about Friday evening – is that an inconvenient time? Say six-thirty – and we'll have a little something to eat afterwards.'

Mandy was doubtful: Tom stayed on Friday evenings for an hour or so. Still, it would be a pity to miss.

'I'll come just for a housewarming drink,' she said.

'Good,' he said. 'I'll look forward to that.'

A year after the death of her husband, Julia Davenport was packing her bags once again to fly out of Italy and back to Paris, where doubtless her travels would begin all over again. It had been the most boring year of her life, one hotel being much like another, and the men, once you got to know them, equally boring. After a few days in Paris, she thought she might try Chamonix – or Sicily.

This time was a little different. She no longer had Nicole Deschamps with her. She had dismissed her a month ago, having put up with enough of her stupid chatter about the women she had previously worked for and their success with men. No, she was better off on her own.

It was late afternoon as she came through the swing doors of the Hotel Crillon, and she struck, as she always did, an arresting figure. A porter followed carrying her furs, another her Vuitton luggage, and the man sitting idly in the reception area reading his newspaper glanced up, down, then looked again. If he wasn't very much mistaken it was Julia Davenport.

Not much interested him these days, but the sight of Julia Davenport did. No sight nor sound of her for over a year, and here she was in Paris. His large, square face flushed slightly as he wondered how best to approach her. Not now, but later, since she was obviously staying here – but for how long?

His heart quickened with interest, and he felt hot under the collar. He watched as, having booked in, she would obviously be staying here. After she had gone to the lift, he made his way to the reception desk, and on the pretence of collecting his keys and his mail idly read the register upside down. The last entry was, sure enough, Lady Julia Davenport, with an address in Italy. That, he knew was their small private villa. Had she been there all this time?

He went straight to the bar and ordered his drink, taking it to a table where he could see straight through the great doors to the reception area. Later he would have dinner but he wanted to be sure that he did not miss her She was unlikely to go out, having just arrived, but he wasn't going to miss this opportunity.

Just before eight o'clock, he saw her emerge from the lift, looking ravishing. Exquisitely dressed, her head held high, she looked neither to the right nor to the left, but went straight to the dining room, where a waiter led her to a discreet corner, and she would have her back to him, he realised, when he took his seat.

No matter – he would know when she left, and it was at that point that he determined to speak to her.

Her back straight, hair perfectly coiffed, her slim arms, and her beautiful hands with their dark painted nails, the rings flashing – oh, yes, it was Julia all right. Where had she been all this time? He had caught a glimpse of that expressionless face but strangely enough the cold expression did nothing to spoil her beauty; rather enhanced it. Her face might have been carved out of marble.

He ate his meal, his mind on other things, and when he had finished took his coffee in the coffee lounge, which he knew she would have to pass through. If she didn't stop, he would accost her. Yes, quite openly. If she sat for coffee, so much the better. He was playing a waiting game, but speak to her he would.

She came through from the dining room and took her seat on one of the soft single armchairs with a table before it. Only when the waiter arrived with the coffee did she move, to pick up the cup. The coffee was black and strong, and she looked straight in front of her.

She was still beautiful, he thought, but then women don't lose that kind of classical beauty. And those wonderful eyes – she could be blind for all it mattered, so dead was the expression in them.

He got up at once, and made his way across to her. She was forced to look up at the dark shadow in front of her, and he saw a flicker in those eyes.

'Jack Leadbetter,' he said softly. 'Julia?' He saw that he had startled her, but her composure was excellent.

'Jack,' she said. 'Jack Leadbetter.'

'May I?' he asked, and brought a chair alongside hers before she had time to object. Well, he decided, she's not the woman she was, but then I'm not the Jack Leadbetter I was. We are two different people.

She said nothing for a while, and quietly sipped her coffee, then she asked him, 'Susan not with you?'

'Susan? Oh, well, of course, you've been away – Susan and I are divorced.'

This did register and her eyes widened.

'I'm sorry, I didn't know.'

'Why be sorry?' he asked. 'It was inevitable.' And I'll tell her, he thought, if it's the last thing I do. She's so bloody placid, looks as if nothing could touch her – leaving those girls – clearing off like that. Susan may have had the morals of an alley cat but she was warm; this woman is like ice. She cares only for herself. Jack was a simple man; there was nothing devious about him.

They drank their coffee, saying nothing. Then he turned to her. 'I always like a little stroll after a meal,' and he saw her frown. 'It's a lovely evening, Julia – want to come?'

He saw she was about to say no, then she took a deep breath. 'Well – a little way – a breath of fresh air.'

'That's it,' he agreed. 'Shall I get you a wrap?'

'No – I'll be fine,' and she drew the soft silken scarf which matched her dress around her shoulders.

They walked out of the swing doors and

into the streets of Paris, the soft night air about them. Presently he took her arm and she made no demur, but seemed rather grateful.

She was only a little thing, he thought, feeling a momentary outrage against Dennis and what he had got up to. It couldn't have been easy; still–

They walked silently until they reached the Seine, and they stood looking down into the dark waters, with brilliant lights everywhere and river boats and lovers, Notre Dame standing high and proud. I came here with Susan, he thought; but it was difficult to know what Julia was thinking. It always had been.

She shivered slightly.

'Shall we go back?' he asked.

She nodded.

They walked back slowly, Jack having said none of the things he had meant to say.

Once inside the hotel, it was warm, and he made straight for the sumptuously furnished lounge. She sat on one of the soft sofas. 'I think we need something cheering,' he said. 'A brandy?'

'Please.'

After the waiter had brought the brandies and she had taken a sip, he decided the time had come. 'Well, what have you been doing with yourself?' He wouldn't chide her, wouldn't criticise her; only she knew why she had done what she had.

'Travel, mostly,' she said, as if she was unused to speaking.

'And where have you been – anywhere interesting?' He tried to sound light, mildly curious.

'All over, Italy, Switzerland, Venice–'

'Is Venice still as beautiful?'

'I suppose,' she said languidly. 'I didn't care for it as much as I used to.'

'Well – you and I are not the same people, Julia.'

She turned to look at him. 'What are you doing here?'

'I had a spot of business to do, then I thought I'd stay on for a couple of days. And you?'

She took a deep breath. 'A stopping-off ground, before I–'

'Whizz off again?' he asked.

'Yes – I expect so.'

No good asking after the girls – they hadn't heard from her. She was always a selfish bitch, he thought, but looking at her saw that she was also vulnerable, and what she had learned that day at the funeral would have given some women a nervous breakdown. But then it had, in a way...

'Julia,' he said. 'Isn't it time you faced up to a few facts?' After all, he had nothing to lose.

She looked coldly at him. 'I'm better not knowing,' she said. 'I've already learned enough to last me a lifetime.'

'Yes,' he said, 'but life goes on,' and took the plunge. 'Did you know that Susan was or had been Dennis' mistress?'

'I suspected,' she said calmly.

'You mean–'

'Jack, you can't be married to someone like Dennis and not know.' And she knew it was the first time she had said Dennis's name out loud since he died. 'Susan adored him.' She looked at him. 'All women did. Poor Jack.'

'I had no idea, until it all came out – over this other chap.'

'People like Susan – and Dennis – should never marry. They can't stay faithful.'

'But if you knew, why did you–'

'I never realised how many – there were so many – and then of course–'

'The boy?'

'Please don't talk about it, Jack. I can't bear it.'

Now the violet eyes were full of tears, and he welcomed them. No one could see them, and wouldn't have cared if they had. This was Paris, where emotions were not something to be ashamed of.

'But I held on to him – all those years.' It was proudly said.

She stared ahead. Yes, he thought, with all your little illnesses, your little dramas, Dennis always thought you were so frail, like a broken flower – had to be taken care of, while he lusted after other women ... sick kind of life, Jack thought.

And now, her face seemed to crumple, and she reached for her handbag and her hankie.

'I'm sorry, Jack. Forgive me–'

'Look,' he said. 'Let's take you to your room.'

She made no demur when he took her arm, and they went over to the lift. Once inside the room, he poured her a cool drink of iced water. 'Drink this,' he said.

Now, the violet eyes had a trace of warmth in them as she looked at him.

'Oh, Jack, you don't know–'

'I can imagine,' he said. 'Don't talk anymore.'

She sat on the *chaise-longue*. 'I think I am

going to faint.'

'No, you're not,' Jack said, causing her to open her eyes wide. 'You're strong, Julia, and don't you forget it. You may not look it, but you're tough, and you know, that's something to be proud of, isn't it?'

She got up and went over to the window, and she stared out into the lovely courtyard, where a fountain played and tubs of flowers shone their colours in the gleaming night lights.

'I'm going home at the weekend, Julia,' he said. 'Will you come with me?'

She turned, startled, then her shoulders sagged. It was as if she suddenly collapsed inwardly.

She smiled at him. A lovely smile. 'Yes, Jack, I will.'